A Hidden War

*Occult Operations Against
Nazi Germany*

Chris Chilcott

A Hidden War
Occult Operations Against
Nazi Germany

Copyright © *Chris Chilcott,* 2025
All Rights Reserved

ISBN:

Also by the Author:

A Killing A Day: Supplying the British Army, 1793 to 1815

Table of Contents

Notes from the Real World

No modern nation has been as strongly associated with the occult as Nazi Germany. A large section of popular culture has evolved around the tropes of Nazi flying saucers, magic and creatures drawn from folklore. This has been fueled by conspiracy theories and misinterpretation about the technology and science of Nazi Germany. Yet, within this, there are facts. At its heart, Nazism was an ideology based on corrupted ideas around mysticism and folklore. Much of Nazi symbology, most infamously the Swastika and SS lightning bolts, were taken from folklore. Senior Nazis sought occult artefacts and consulted astrologers. There were mystical societies, and archaeological expeditions were dispatched to remote parts of the world.

It was not only in the sphere of the arcane that links can be drawn between the Nazis and the occult. In sections of Western culture, there exists a focus on the *wunderwaffen* (wonder weapons) of Nazi Germany. Jet fighters, advanced submarines and rockets are among their perceived scientific and technical leads. In fact, there were many areas in which the Allies were more advanced, but these were far less spectacular than those of the Nazis. Taken in isolation, Nazi weapon developments seem to veer into science fiction. This is particularly so when proposals for supersonic stratospheric bombers and space-based weapons are considered. The fact that the Allies were in competition to retrieve German technology at the war's end further fuels the concept of Nazi Germany being far ahead of the Allies technologically. 'Advanced' German aircraft designs, combined with the explosion of interest in UFOs in the 1950s, led to the idea that the Nazis had help from off the planet to achieve their technological lead. It is somewhat ironic that while the Allies split the atom, pioneered computers and also had operational jet fighters; it was the Germans who must have had help from extra-terrestrials.

If the Nazis had indeed been aided by extra-terrestrials; if they had been successful in their search for the magical artefacts of lost civilizations; if the creatures of myth and folklore were real: what would the response of the Allies have been? Central to the Allied victory in World War II was the cycle of development and counter-measure. The Germans deployed U-boats, the Allies deployed convoys. New German radars were jammed and tactics developed to counter new weapon systems. Commandos, resistance groups and bombing raids were used to disrupt projects such as V weapon production and nuclear research. Finally, there were the sledgehammer options of massed produced weapons and the atomic bomb. The Allies could simply bring more firepower to bear. There is no reason to doubt that the Allies may have responded in similar ways to Nazi efforts in the paranormal field.

In a scenario in which the Nazis knew of the occult, so too would the Allies and the other Axis powers. They, too, would have had occult forces. Yet, if the occult was real and acknowledged, the world would be a vastly different place. So different that it is likely World War II as we know it would never happen. Therefore, while real, the occult remains hidden, dismissed as superstition, ignored in the name of logic or knowledge of its existence suppressed. Perhaps we live in such a world. What if there was indeed an occult war fought between the Allies and Nazi Germany, a war about which the general populace remains ignorant. A hidden war. This is a work of fictional history. It is not a novel. It is not an alternative history in its true sense.

Nothing changes; all of history's events happen with the same outcomes. The Germany Blitzkrieg against the west is successful; the Soviet Union is invaded, Pearl Harbor is bombed, and D-Day happens on 6 June 1944. In short the events leading up to our world are no different, but shaped by occult warfare in ways we are unaware. This is an exploration of occult warfare as it may have occurred. A war waged in the shadows, unknown to populations and maybe even their governments.

Only a handful of real people feature significantly in this work. Among them are Heinrich Himmler, with his deranged and twisted occult views, Vidkun Quisling. The Norwegian collaborator did not have strong occult credentials. Nonetheless he does fulfill a role in a narrative about the use of Norse mythology for nationalistic purposes. It has been impossible not to reference Alistair Crowley. Crowley was an occultist, adventurer, and, allegedly, a British intelligence agent. In short, he would have played a key role in the occult war. The Russian monk Rasputin was long dead by World War II. Yet he is surrounded by mythology and was an occultist who was at the heart of the Tsarist Russian state. Thus, he would have likely played a part in the development of occult warfare. Another historical figure referenced is Air Marshal Hugh Dowding. The leader of RAF fighter command during the Battle of Britain, Dowding, had what can be considered as occult beliefs. He was both a believer in the philosophy of theosophy and a spiritualist. Finally, there is Rudolf Hess. Hess was Hitler's deputy and flew to Scotland in 1941 allegedly to negotiate peace between Germany and Britain. The incident remains surrounded by mystery and intrigue, with rumors of Hess later being replaced by a body double.

A number of real-life events are also mentioned and given an occult slant. This in no way intended to denigrate the seriousness of the events, those who lost their lives or the people involved. The events include the destruction of the airship R101 in 1930, the bombing of Coventry, the sinking of HMS Glorious and a number of real-life battles and campaigns. Some events are mentioned that remain shrouded in mystery and conspiracy theories. These include the so-called 'Battle of Shingle Street' and the sinking of HMS Glorious. It is highly likely the no military engagement actually happened at Shingle Street, despite an urban legend of a failed German landing attempt. The Shingle Street myth also links to rumors of charred German corpses washing up on the European coastline after the British 'set fire to the sea' to repel an invasion.[1] The loss of the escort carrier HMS Dasher was indeed sunk with significant loss of life. Remarkably, efforts were made to keep its sinking secret until after the war. The cause of its loss remains contested (although likely a design flaw covered up for political reasons), and there are reports of mass graves for the crew, a fact denied by the Royal Navy.

A Hidden War uses a definition of the occult that is a broad one. It encompasses magic, psychic powers, mythical creatures, cryptids, pseudoscience and extra-terrestrials. Extra-terrestrials may have their own forms of magic and worship their own gods. There are ancient horrors aplenty, but no zombies. I never got the whole zombie genre. Spirits are defined as incorporeal beings that were once living, this includes ghosts, wraiths and poltergeists. Entities is a term to

---

[1] That the Germans would secretly launch an invasion, and the British keep its defeat secret, is perhaps the most absurd conspiracy theory arising from WWII.

refer to a variety of intelligent creatures not of this earth that can be summoned. Many may popularly referred to as demons but may include creatures worshipped as deities. Lycans generally refer to werewolves, werebeasts for other types. Finally, there is the fae. This refers to all manner of lesser magical creatures such as faeries, mer beings, pixies and Yeti. As befits the focus of this work, the focus is on the mythology and folklore of northern Europe. It has also been impossible to resist the cliché of explaining real-life events, mysteries or urban legends through occult happenings. A bonus point for each one that you identify.

The Divide

From this point a possibly fictional history begins. Here there be monsters…

Shoulder Patch worn by members of Vortigern Organisation, 1943 to 1945

The greatest trick the Devil ever pulled was convincing the world he didn't exist.

- Charles Baudelaire-

Baudelaire was wrong. It was never the devil's trick, nor his intention. Occultists convinced the world, they made it happen because it suited them. The devil had no choice in the matter. It is our role to sustain the ignorance of the population. Ignorance brings protection because it stifles belief in occult matters. The devil is aware, he acquiesces in this. Why? Because there is worse than the devil. I know this because I asked him yesterday.

Address of the Chief Warlock of the Northern Sabbat to the leadership of the Exotic Warfare Executive, 1 September 1939

Abbreviations of Occult Warfare Organisations and Units

(Br: British; Fr: French; US: United States; Ger: German; Sov: Soviet; Du: Dutch)

AC	(Br) Airborne Coven
APIB	(Br) Aerial Phenomena Investigation Branch
AREBaC	(Br) Anglican Rites, Exorcisms and Banishments Committee
AUO	(Du) Afdeling voor Uitgebreide Oorlogsvoering (translated Department for Extended Warfare)
Btl.SJ	(Ger) Battalion Schattenjäger (trans. Dark Hunter) (Wehrmacht)
CBB	(Sov) специальное военное ведомство – (trans. Special Warfare Agency)
CLWD	(Br) Conventional Land Warfare Directorate
DExNA	(US) Department of Extra-normal Affairs
EACAC	(Br) EWE Air Combat Advisory Committee
EOG	(Br) Esoteric Operations Group
EWE	(Br) Exotic Warfare Executive
GDG	(Br) General Defence Group
ICG	(Br) Imperial Coven Group
NZL	(Ger) Nachtzerstörer-Legion (trans. Night Destroyer Legion) (Luftwaffe)
O.Abt.K.	(Ger) Ozean-Abteilung Krake (trans. Ocean Battalion Kraken) (Kriegsmarine)
OOE	(Br) Occult Operations Executive, semiofficial but widely name of SOE's occult Apollo Section. Used in this work to refer to the organisation.
RMOWU	(Br) Royal Marine Occult Warfare Unit
SOEAS	(Br) Official designation of SOE's Apollo Section
SS. BdN	(Ger) SS Battalion Night Walker
SS.Kp.K	(Ger) S.S. Kompanie Kralle
UAMS	(Fr) Unités d'assaut en milieu sauvage (wilderness assault units)

ZaS	(Ger) Zerkel auf See (Covens at Sea) (Kriegsmarine)

Military Abbreviations

BEF	British Expeditionary Force
INA	Indian National Army
IJA	Imperial Japanese Army
IJN	Imperial Japanese Navy
RAF	Royal Air Force
RFC	Royal Flying Corps
RNAS	Royal Navy Air Service
USAAF	United States Army Air Force

Tables

Introduction:
Preparations for Occult warfare

Britain has a long tradition of mysticism and occult activity. The ancient druids called on spirits to aid them against the Roman invaders, who in turn used Celtic seers to supplement their own. Kings and queens found a use for occultists in their courts. Entities and various creatures were employed against Catholics and Protestants, depending on who was, or rather not, in the ascendency during the sixteenth century.

The occult was a constant thread running through the history of Britain, but it was also a hidden one. The pre-Christian and early medieval populations of Britain were alike in being especially knowledgeable about occult matters. Ironically, this is now dismissed as superstition and ignorance but it was a knowledge that contemporary ruling elites recognized. Pacts with dark forces were necessary to preserve the status of rulers, yet these were pacts that they would dare not admit to for fear of provoking popular unrest. The origins of the concept of divine right emerged as a means of explaining occult interventions as acts of god. This was an arrangement convenient to practitioners of the occult and magical beings. There was a suspicion of mystics and practitioners of magic that forced them to remain unseen, concealed amongst the ranks of court officials and advisors. It was a mutually beneficial arrangement, safeguarding the reputation of kings while keeping occultists safe through anonymity, lest the more powerful become targets of rival factions or the prey of occult entities.

The races of the fae, including pixies, faeries and aquatic merfolk, sought to remain detached from mortal affairs.[2] Being long lived, such creatures had much to lose. They also had a tendency to wait patiently, aloof and uninvolved through the successive crises caused by mortal conflicts. Their paranoia was heightened by scientific and technological advances. The fae recognized that these advances offered mortals capabilities that would surpass their own mystically derived ones. Thus mortals were a growing threat, a fact sensed by the various creatures that derived their essence from the same energies as the mystics of the fae. Growing human encroachment into the untamed wildernesses further emphasized this.

The desire for occultists to remain hidden, alongside the paranoia of occult beings, created a situation in which the occult became invisible. Its influence waxed and waned, but it was an underlying current in human existence. By the nineteenth century, the occult had become a secret state within a state. It was a hidden stratum of society whose practitioners had the same whims and desires as those who went about in ignorance. Unlike occult beings, occultists soon found their causes enhanced by science. They allowed science to debunk or dismiss the occult, facilitating a deepening of their obscurity. It was not unknown for scientific endeavors to be covertly sponsored by occult groups for this purpose.

In 1902 growing tensions between the powers prompted the Exotic Warfare Executive to be established. An obscure

---

[2] These were just those fae creatures prevalent in Northern and Western Europe. Due to their physical nature but magical essence the Sasquatch of North America are also categorised as such. The term fae has also been erroneously extended to Djinn but these, unlike the fae, are most frequently incorporeal beings.

sub-department of a seemingly minor section of an intelligence organisation, EWE, was funded by occultists to further national interests. Such groups were not unknown. The Royal Navy was covertly supported by a secret occult society that had existed in various forms since the reign of Henry VIII.

Similarly, groups of like-minded cultists, sometimes individuals, had informally supported military campaigns. However, such activities had been short lived. Many lasted, at most, only a few months, groups dispersing due to redeployment, fear of ridicule and persecution by colleagues or the threat of hostile occultists and entities.

The initial membership of EWE was drawn from an occult group known as the Southwest Midlands Esoteric Society. Its members included civil servants, bankers, lawyers and military officers, retired and serving. The influence of the society stretched across the Empire and beyond. This gave EWE access to a large pool of occultists and mystics from a number of traditions, and it retained a significant Hindu influence into the 1960s.

The field force of EWE was Excalibur. Its principal role was intelligence gathering, but sections or platoons could be formed for 'intensive', i.e. combat operations. Its operatives were highly trained but did not possess mystic or similar abilities. Individuals possessing such aptitudes would have been utilised within other departments. For non-covert field operations, Excalibur operatives wore army-style uniforms and equipment. Excalibur operatives were among the few EWE personnel to regularly wear uniforms.

The Elite Vortigern group was formed by EWE in 1913 to counter entities employed by enemy forces. Its covens were expected to be deployed to the front lines and thus wore a uniform. Viewed as an elite force, Vortigern was made independent of EWE in 1917 so that it would be able to develop tactics unhindered by other operational demands. As a result of its growth, the EWE was divided into a number of departments (or offices). These are shown below in Figure 1.

Department	Role
B Office	Scandinavian, Arctic and Baltic affairs
C Office	Aerial warfare (beasts and aircraft)
E Office	Mystic and extra-terrestrial diplomatic relations
G Office	Psychic infiltration
H Office	Domestic security
M Office	Maritime Operations
R Office	Artefacts
T Office	Far East
Excalibur	Non-mystic field agents
Vortigern	Counter entity & spirit warfare

Figure 1: The largest EWE Departments, 1916

The departments themselves coordinated activities and provided specialists, but personnel were not permanent. Specific occult abilities were frequently required for operations, and the number of suitably able personnel was small. The result was movement between departments and even organisations. It is likely that at any one time, as many as 70% of EWE's occultists could be considered freelance, and foreigners were common. This was particularly so after the 1917 Russian Revolution, which forced many of that nation's most gifted occultists to emigrate.

EWE was a decentralized organisation. Its departments were headquartered in locations across Britain and overseas. These included stately homes, farms and townhouses. This was consequence of the need for EWE operatives to be located in locations that enabled them to draw upon different sources of magical energy. These sources included stone circles, portals, ley lines and sites sacred to the fae. Conveniently, the dispersal of the organisation to obscure locations also reduced its visibility to the wider population. Decentralization was also a feature of the departments themselves. Excalibur, in particular operated as a network of operatives, some associating themselves with specific offices or geographic areas. The precise nature of EWE's leadership structure remains an enigma. Various committees and bodies held sway at various times. It may be that this was deliberate to ensure too much power was never invested within one group. Equally, it may reflect that the occult abilities within any group of individuals could wax and wane.

By 1907, organisations similar to EWE had arisen in nations such as France, the Netherlands, Russia and Germany. Like EWE, these organisations were decentralized. However, those of Germany and Russia, in particular, were able to maintain a small number of specialized facilities in remote areas of their home countries. This included a number of castles in Germany that would later become closely associated with the Nazi regime.[3]

In 1911 saw the creation of the US Naval Surveillance Department 14. This would merge with the US Army's 'Prairie Wendigo' organisation in 1922, creating the Department for Extra-Normal Affairs (DExNA) emerged. What prompted the creation of such groups within the space of a few years is unclear. Indeed, such was their secretive nature it is possible that one or more had emerged before EWE. It has also been theorized that the efforts of EWE to

---

[3] The lack of similar wilderness locations had a direct impact on EWE's attempts to make covert contact with alien delegations arriving on Earth.

recruit mystics had drawn attention to the concept, prompting others to follow. The discovery of Atlantis by a private French expedition in 1898, an event unknown outside of a handful of individuals, may also have played a part in encouraging the ambitions of occultists.

The creation of national organisations to pursue occult warfare has been attributed to a natural response to such threats against the backdrop of an arms race. A much darker hypothesis is that in their collective subconscious, occultists across the world had witnessed what was to come in the years following 1914. If this was truly the case, they were, for the most part, ill-prepared. The technology of war proved to be capable of destroying all but the most powerful wards. Enchanters, sigils and lycans were blasted into oblivion. Neither did bullets and shells discriminate between those with occult gifts and those without. Only in Russia, under the direction of Rasputin, was any notable success achieved. It was Rasputin's fate and those of the Romanovs whom he sought to protect that served to underline the importance of EWE's continued secret existence.

Several occult organisations were created to support British military operations during World War I. These were influenced by EWE and included the British Army's Esoteric Operations Committee (later Group) and the Royal Flying Corps' Air Phenomena Investigations Branch, known as APIB. In 1917, members of sabbats from across the British Empire created the Imperial Coven Group. This had been created in response to what they perceived as EWE's encroachment on their activities but the two organisations cooperated closely. The premier British occult combat was the Royal Marine Occult Warfare Unit (RMOWU). This had existed in various forms since 1790 but expanded to platoon strength in 1917.

Total war had brought a new danger for occultists. Should they be discovered, their utilization by states to meet war aims was inevitable. Thus, during the interwar period organisations such as EWE sought to continue their obscurity whilst preparing for the next conflict. They continued to operate at the very fringes of the state. Many of those individuals who funded EWE or shielded it from public knowledge had their own ambitions in the political sphere. They recognized the influence an organisation such as EWE could bring, enabling it to continue to operate in obscurity. Such was the nature of its operations that outsiders intent on revealing its operations would be dismissed as insane, blackmailed or otherwise neutralized.

The decade following World War I was characterized by minimal occult threat within Britain. The war had disrupted the flow of magical energies. Wicca, druids and other practitioners of folk magic found the fae, their traditional partners, withdrawing into isolation after being appalled by the carnage of the Western Front. Familiars, lesser fae beings that were conduits of magical energies, became increasingly rare. Only the fields of mediumship and spiritualism offered a viable outlet for occultists. This was fueled by a growing desire amongst the public to contact deceased family members and loved ones lost in the war. Such activities were relatively benign, although there remained the ever-present danger that those dabbling in occult matters could accidentally summon malicious spirits.

Whether due to the desire to escape the war, explore new ideologies or an effort to establish their own followers, many of the more dangerous occultists had established themselves overseas. It was the role of EWE to police such individuals in the Empire and Dominions, and they did so effectively. Many would-be cult leaders found themselves incarcerated in colonial prisons, executed or victim to the beings they had summoned. The result of these changes to occult practices in the decade following enabled EWE to focus on defending Britain from external threats. Those originating within its borders increasingly became the focus of the Anglican Rites and Banishments Committee (AREBaC), or MI5's so-called Guinevere Group.

During the 1920s, it seemed likely that EWE's next opponents could well be the occult forces of France. These had been restructured from 1918 into so-called 'gemstone departments'.

Dept.	Branch	Role
Ruby	Navy	Maritime operations. Security of Atlantis.
Emerald	Army-Navy	Mystical intelligence gathering.
Sapphire	Army	Mystic warfare
Jade	Navy/Air Force	Study of Extra-terrestrials
Onyx	Navy	Diplomatic relations with the fae and contacts with entities

Figure 2: The Principal French Gemstone Departments, 1926.

These departments sought to utilise the mystic resources of France and its Empire while exploiting the knowledge gained from Atlantis. It was at the time of increased tensions with France that EWE made the decision to distance itself from overt involvement with extra-terrestrials. EWE was a conservative organisation and believed that off-world forces were a distraction from the occult. It was a decision that sought to enable EWE to focus on maximizing the occult potential of the British Isles and Empire. It was also a short-sighted decision. One that would have a detrimental impact on Britain's occult warfare capability into the twenty-first century.

While France's so called gemstone departments received a scant trickle of government support, the more occult-orientated Nazi government of Germany in the 1930s actively funded research. This funding was carefully concealed, and the extent to which senior figures, including Hitler, were involved is disputed. Whatever the case, all branches of the German armed forces had occult programmes of various sizes. Like those of the British and French, these were highly secretive.

Italy, Germany's partner in the European Axis, adopted a different approach to that of the other powers in the occult warfare field. Italian occult warfare organisations, such as the navy's Caelus Extra-Terrestrial Diplomatic Team and Trident, were extremely small but highly integrated even across the arms of service. This enabled resources to be effectively pooled for specific projects. However, these were relatively small in number and unambitious compared to those of the other powers.

The most significant of Germany's occult research organisations were the Ahnenerbe of the SS and the Thule Society. The latter was independent of any military organisation and provided advisors. The SS Black Sun group was focused almost entirely and extra-terrestrials, and there existed a number of SS projects that were ambitious in scope but proved a significant drain on resources. The Luftwaffe, Wehrmacht and Kriegsmarine also conducted their own research. The German occult effort was characterized by competition and rivalry. Despite this shortcoming, the broad scope of research gave Nazi Germany the potential to use its occult capabilities to turn the war in its favor. It was a challenge that EWE had been preparing to face.

Chapter 1

Spirit and Beast Warfare

By May 1939, it was increasingly evident that Hitler would not back down over his demands concerning Poland. Neither could the British or French provide direct military aid in the event of a German invasion. Other than allied offensives in the West, it seemed that Poland would be left to fend for itself. Nevertheless, whilst conventional military options to support Poland were limited, it was apparent that mystical and occult warfare had the potential to be more decisive. Mystics located in Western Europe could be used to provide long-range support, including limited offensive activity and, importantly, had the potential to summon or enhance beings and entities within Poland. Like many nations Poland contained denizens of its dark forests and other wild places that could be enticed to resist an invader. Amongst the most powerful of these were the various vampiric creatures, including the Crimson Vampires. Therefore, in June 1939, a EWE diplomatic team, codenamed Taurus and consisting of a number of influential occultists, travelled to the Balkans and Eastern Europe. Their mission was to liaise with Poland's occult community and to gain the support of the vampire clans.

Taurus' mission would prove to be a failure. The undertaking was based on a serious misreading of the situation, a dramatic underestimation of the rapid decline in the power of the vampire clans since the nineteenth century. Western mystics had long been in awe of the vampire clans, but this power was merely a façade. Centuries of inbreeding between vampires, humans and other occult beings had diluted the bloodlines to such a point that many clans were little more than mystically gifted mortals. The ability of the descendants of Dracul to walk in the sunlight was not mastery of weakness but the result of the near complete removal of vampiristic traits. The last remnants of vampire power had been swept away in the carnage of World War I. Centuries of accumulated wealth had helped to mask the decline of the clans, perhaps aided by the infiltration of organisations such as EWE and Emerald.

That the decline of vampire influence had been unnoticed by British and French occult agencies was itself a failure. Worse was that the decline was abundantly clear to the Soviet's primary occult warfare organisation, **специальное военное ведомство** (Special Warfare Agency), known as the CBB. American mystic Tudor Hallum, a founder of DExNA, wrote in 1949 that:

> The British failure to appreciate the decline of vampire clans was perhaps their greatest failure in the occult sphere of the 1930s. The Soviets had been exterminating vampires within their borders with impunity since 1925, and the Vatican had almost ceased to recognize them as a threat as early as 1919. EWE was looking to the past for solutions to modern problems and failing. By ignoring truly powerful occult beings in the region, EWE had allowed the Soviets to expand their influence. It would be a foothold that we would be powerless to counter in the early Cold War years.

The Taurus team returned to Poland without the support of the vampire clans. This was in part due to apathy on the part of the clans and also due to the realization that it would have, in any case, counted for very little. Even the most noble of the clan leaders could boast no more control over the vampire creatures of Poland than any moderately powerful mystic. In its final report, the leader of the Taurus mission noted:

> the family of Dracul has been reduced to a gentlemen's club for a blood-drinking cult. Debauchery of all kinds abounds, but for occult strength, we must look elsewhere.

It was a message acted on by both EWE and France's Sapphire Organisation.

Sapphire had been created in 1929 in response to German efforts aimed at using spirits for military purposes. In 1922, Hans Kelhoff, a Captain in the German army, had made the first steps towards this form of warfare when attempting to resurrect his platoon, which had been wiped out by French shelling in 1917. Like many others in the aftermath of World War I, Kelhoff had become interested in spiritualism but combined this with Prussian militarism, eastern philosophy and a desire to avenge Germany's defeat. Kelhoff's initial experiment met with mixed results, and rather than summoning old comrades he found himself confronted by a number of angered spirits. Many of these had become restless in their search for a gateway to the afterlife. Only swift intervention by the two Tibetan mystics who had joined Kelhoff prevented the incident from turning deadly. Yet Kelhoff had not only contacted fallen heroes. He had also witnessed their destructive potential.

Through his mystical associates, Kelhoff made contact with the Turkish spiritualist Hazal Bilgic. The great-granddaughter of an alleged necromancer, Bilgic, had risen to prominence in occult circles after using spirits to spy on Allied forces during the Gallipoli campaign. Bilgic's skills, combined with selected Nordic runes, enabled Kelhoff to summon and control small groups of spirits. Through his Tibetan mentors, he was also increasingly able to select the type of spirits summoned. The activities of Kelhoff and Bilgic were being increasingly noted in occult circles. Hallum wrote to a fellow U.S. mystic in 1924:

> the prowess of Kelhoff and his Turk princess grows daily. It was only two nights ago that they summoned four poltergeists from the fallen of the 1918 German army. The ability to select the nature of the spirit summoned is most impressive and far outstrips the chance of the encounters to which I am accustomed. I fear, however, that the intention is far from good but very much malign.

Hallum was evidently impressed and appalled in equal measure, the latter feeling justified by subsequent developments.

Kelhoff found supporters in the German army. Such individuals were driven, it seems, by revenge, genuine spiritualism, and the desire to create forces that fell outside the scope of the hated Treaty of Versailles. Tanks and planes were restricted, the spirits of the fallen not so. Limited trials were first conducted by Kelhoff's so-called '*Geist Korps*' in 1926 and drew the attention of occultists assigned to French intelligence. Experiments continued, and by 1933, there existed three *Geist Korps* in the German army. In 1935 one of these would be allocated to the SS and based in the Black Forest while a second was granted to the Luftwaffe in 1938.

The latter would last only 6 months longer due to its spirits being sacrificed in a failed attempt to summon a host of Valkyries as part of Operation Wotan.

By the summer of 1937, the Nazis' mastery of spirits had reached the point at which they were, albeit covertly, able to support conventional military forces. At this time, the Nazis remained anxious not to breach the Bermuda Treaty of 1921, which forbade the deployment of magic and other esoteric forces against human opponents. Thus the concept was to be tested by reconnaissance operations in support of Spanish Nationalists. However, spirit warfare detachment *Gabel* (Pitchfork) would engage in limited combat operations against the small number of lycans operated in Spain by the Soviet CBB.

Like Nazi Germany, the USSR had taken the opportunity to trial its own occult warfare units in the conflict and had deployed a variety of creatures, primarily wolves but also bears and an eagle, all bound by a Siberian shaman. Unlike the Nazis, the Soviets had shown a willingness to ignore the terms of the Bermuda Treaty and had unleashed its CBB assets in a campaign of terror behind Nationalist lines. Ironically, the brutality of the attacks served Nationalist propaganda, which blamed them on Republican or Anarchist terror tactics.

The threat posed by the Soviet's lycans needed to be neutralized, and this provided an opportunity to deploy *Gabel'* on combat duties. In October 1937 a party of mystics led by Bilgic summoned a particularly powerful and vindictive kinetic spirit, thought to be a victim of the 16th Century Inquisition. Assaulting the camp, two of the CBB's creatures were crushed by a storm of boulders whilst in human form. A third was half a mile into a nearby deep valley. Bilgic's own coven finished the creature and slew the

CBB personnel present in the camp. It is claimed that the mutilated remains were later used in a ceremony to honor the deity Moloch and that at least one Soviet operative was sacrificed in the process. The incident caused alarm in the Ahnenerbe, who sought to develop a controllable occult warfare capability. SS Colonel Johannes Arndt wrote a scathing report to his superiors about the activities of *Gabel* andthe wasted opportunities to acquire tissue samples of Soviet creatures and extract intelligence from captured human assets. The final *Gabel* unit was not stood down until August 1941, after the final CBB detachments in Spain had been neutralized.

Sapphire had not been idle during this period and had been able to observe many of the *Geist Korps'* activities in Spain with relative ease. The Nazis' mystics in Spain employed only rudimentary warding that prevented scrying but little else. Madagascan divination spells proved particularly effective and were able to completely shield astral projection into the *Geist Korps* Spanish headquarters on three separate occasions. The projections were carried out by the Quebecoise mystic and Sapphire operative Jean-Phillippe Picard. Located in Toulouse Picad projected into the headquarters for the first time on 23 January 1937 and was spotted by a sentry whilst in astral form, the sentry believing Picad's form to be a spirit summoned by the *Gabel* team. Picad was able to ascertain the composition of the *Gabel* team, including the presence of Bilgic and Tibetan mystics.

This valuable information obtained by Picad was supplemented on his second projection on 17 March. During this Picad was able to commit to memory a 250-page Tibetan manuscript using a retainment enchantment. The third and final projection into the headquarters occurred in

June when Picad was able to conduct surveillance on a meeting between high-ranking members of Italy's Operation Lilith, Colonel Arndt of the Ahnenerbe and the *Geist Korps*. Picad was able to report back on the clear mistrust between the Ahnenerbe and the *Geist Korps*, as well as confirm much of what was already known about Lilith. A fourth attempt by Picad was postponed when it became apparent that more effective wards had been implemented by the *Geist Korps* upon the urging of the Ahnenerbe.

The intelligence gained by Picad had proved invaluable. It confirmed suspected divisions between the mystical organisations of the Reich that the Allies would exploit throughout the coming war. More significant was that information contained within his memories of the manuscript seen in March. So much information was retained in so short a time (all 250 pages in a language unknown to Picad within a mere ten minutes) that it had to be retained deep in his subconscious. This feat, and the lengthy process to retrieve it, physically and mentally damaged Picad to the extent that he would retire from field operations, bed-bound and living just long enough to see the end of the war, passing in his sleep on 17 October 1945, aged 29.

The Frenchman's sacrifice would not be in vain, as the manuscript had been the key to Kelhoff and Bilgic's success. The agents of EWE and Sapphire had been able to successfully summon spirits since the 1920s but the outcome had very much been one of chance. Spirits summoned could be malign, benign or anything in between. Experiments conducted in Hampshire during the 1930s had resulted in an angry French knight, confused infant and jovial merchant all making an appearance during one summoning. Kelhoff's text had opened the door to selecting the nature of the spirit desired.

Like Kelhoff, EWE's leadership favored spirits more suited for combat roles. Unlike EWE, Sapphire advocated a more restrained policy. This was based on the recognition that occult warfare in all its forms remained unreliable and that priority targets would likely be well protected by wards and similar enchantments. It was also apparent that those initiating assassination by spirits summoned from across the seas risked a cycle of increasingly brutal murders once such defenses could be overcome. If one side became proficient at remote murder, would a spirit-based apocalypse be unleashed on civilians in cities? Far better, it was argued, to utilise spirits for surveillance and developing frontline capabilities where they could more easily be countered and controlled by focusing resources.

Besides the practicalities of spirit warfare, there were also diplomatic concerns. French occultists were in negotiation with several fae Kingdoms, many of whom were anxious to avoid the breaking down of the boundaries between realities. These boundaries protected their lands from humans and hostile entities alike. The Dryads of the Brocéliande Forest were particularly fearful of this had had made moves to form a league of neutrality amongst the fae of Western Europe. For EWE, it was the threat of fae neutrality that persuaded them to adopt a less active stance in regard to the use of spirit assassination. Operation Tidal Wave was making good progress, and this was deemed as vital to British mystical interests.[4] As a result, representatives of Britain, France, and the Western European fae Kingdoms signed an agreement at

---

[4] See Chapter 2 'Hammer of a God'.

Carnac on 3 March 1938. By the terms of the Treaty of Carnac:

1. The Allies would not adopt a policy of mass or regular assassination by spirits.
2. Efforts would be made to focus spirit warfare on the battlefield, where they could be better controlled.
3. Allied mystics would be prevented from summoning spirits specified by the fae.
4. To limit damage to boundaries between the human and fae worlds, the Allies would not escalate to match the Nazis' spirit warfare.
5. The fae of Western Europe would support the Allied cause.

Despite the promise made in point 5, the Allies were under no illusions about the loyalty of the fae. It would need to be negotiated, earned and brought if it was to be guaranteed at all. After all, many of the goblins and tricksters of mythology had been fae-kind.

Carnac strengthened negotiations with some of the smaller fae kingdoms. Yet those more independently minded, particularly in Western Britain, hardened against Allied diplomacy. In a handful of cases, fae lords began to become receptive to Axis diplomatic overtures. The French felt satisfied that the British were genuine in their desire to prevent an escalation of spirit warfare. The British, however, had staged a remarkable sleight of hand. Not only did the treaty not impose limits on spirit warfare waged on the battlefield, but plans were already in motion to utilise much darker forces to achieve their goals.

Like Britain, France had recognized that spirit warfare was not the only solution to German developments in this field. To this end, they were pursuing research into so-called

Guerre des Bêtes (War of the Beasts). Sapphire took the lead in research, and Picad's projection in June 1937 confirmed much of what they had already deduced about Axis operations in this field. Italy was very much the senior partner in such activities and had initiated Operation Lilith in 1928. This continued until 1943 and had commenced after Italian archaeologists unearthed ruins in the Libyan Desert. The origins of these ruins remain contentious, and it took many years for the tablets recovered from the site to be deciphered by arcano-archaeologists. The language was an amalgam of middle Sumeria, early Malaysian and *K'lmar* scripts. Intriguingly the latter dated from a time before the first recognized *K'lmar* expeditions to Earth.

It rapidly became apparent that the ruins were a depository for information about numerous species that bore various similarities to canines but also various differences, such as reptilian, avian or non-corporeal forms. Some species dwelt on Earth while others could be summoned. Frustratingly, for the researchers, the information was incomplete and offered no explanation for a number of perfectly spherical chambers alongside the structures in the desert. Nevertheless, it provided sufficient detail to bind or summon a variety of canine-like creatures and entities known to exist in parts of Africa, Europe and Asia.

Like the *Geist Korps*, Lilith's initial wardings were weak, enabling Sapphire and Emerald mystics to remotely view much of Lilith's initial activities, even gaining access to several of the tablets recovered from Libya. By 1932, warding and other countermeasures had been significantly strengthened, but in December 1933, three members associated with Lilith defected to Saphhire. The most important of these defectors was the so-called 'mystic zoologist' Carlo Iachino's role in Lilith had been the summoning and binding of creatures used by the Shetani of East Africa. They themselves were spirits of a highly malevolent nature; the Shetani employed a number of canine species as both guardians and hunters. The most powerful of these creatures were able to project into spirit forms and were reportedly able to track demonic beings. Many in the Italian occult community were aghast at the thought of such creatures being made available, not only to their own fascist regime but also that of Germany with whom Italy was increasingly aligned. Iachino was part of Lilith's operations in Somaliland in early 1933. These operations had wiped out a number of villages by using occult creatures. Amongst these creatures were those of the Shetani. The attacks were completely effective, leaving no survivors, and bloodletting continued as a number of the creatures rampaged through Lilith personnel and a team of SS observers.

The rational course of action would have been to order a temporary halt to further trials but the leadership of Lilith, prompted by observers from the Ahnenerbe and Black Sun organisations, sought to continue. This was too much for Iachino and his Lilith colleagues. The result was their defection. The group brought with them details of the wards used to counter mystic intelligence gathering and information about the creatures used in Somaliland. Amongst the papers was also found information on German research into the use of their own, non-spirit occult creatures. As was often the case, German research had been split across multiple organisations within the German armed forces. Of particular in regard to occult creatures were *S.S. Kompanie Kralle* (SS.Kp.K), the *Wehrmacht's Battalion Schattenjäger* (Btl.SJ) and *Luftwaffe Nachtzerstörer-Legion* (NZL). There were also numerous sub-organisations, including two operated by the Ahnenerbe in Asia and an SS mission in the Balkans, codenamed Gebirgswächter (Mountain Sentinel).

For Sapphire the information supported previous intelligence gathering and also enabled them to accelerate their own activities. French efforts had focused on developing their own lycan formations in the and in camps on the Swiss border. With resources not diverted to multiple projects and knowledge enhanced by the Lilith defectors, Sapphire was able to accelerate its own research. The result was the creation of lycan formations whose mission was twofold: to engage German occult forces such as the *Geist Korps* and to operate behind the lines to track down and terminate enemy mystics.

Being themselves of magical nature, it was expected that the Lycans would also be able to track and engage German spirit forces. Thus, in 1939, despite the failure of Taurus, France felt confident in its ability to counter *Geistkrieg* with its *Guerre des Bêtes* strategy. To maintain secrecy the companies were designated unités d'assaut en milieu sauvage (wilderness assault units) or UAMS. Claremont was a field trials unit with responsibility for evaluating regional lycan types and assessing their usefulness in different environments. As a result, it contained the most diverse range of lycan variants. The 3rd Company was the most controversial, and its existence was kept secret from EWE Formed in 1933, the company's activities included the forced conversion of humans into lycans. Experiments were initially conducted on military prisoners drawn from garrisons in North Africa. By 1935, research had shifted to focus on eugenics with subjects abducted from French colonies. In 1937, a number of Mongolian dissidents were supplied by the Soviet CBB in exchange for data from experiments. The programme was absorbed by the Vichy government but closed down, and its documents were seized by SS.Kp.K in 1942.[5]

Company	Location	Strength
1st	Franco-German border	50
2nd	Franco-Spanish border	22
'Claremont'	Detachments in French-Indo China, Guiana, Syria and Normandy (training).	41
3rd	Franco-Italian border, 'conversion detachment' on Swiss border.	34
'Languedoc'	Franco-German border	17

Figure 3: Deployment of French Lycan companies, 1939[6]

The British counterpart to France's *Guerre des Bêtes* was under the direction of the Armitage Institute. The institute was set up in 1915 by the arcano-archaeologist and mystic Joseph Armitage. Armitage had acquired a considerable archive of arcane materials and artefacts. His focus, however, had been the mystical canine species that dwelt within Britain, particularly the southern moorlands. Armitage vanished on an expedition to the Andes in 1921 and control of the institute passed to his great nephew, James Armitage. He was convinced by Squadron Leader Bentham Elton of the Royal Air Force's APIB that his great uncle's research was vital to the national interest. Armitage was more interested in recent developments in research concerning extra-terrestrial activity conducted by the United States and passed control of the Institute to Elton.

---

[5] A number of researchers travelled to Japan in 1943 via U-boat where they continued their work in China.
[6] Shown in order of formation, the 1st being formed as a cadre in 1928.

By 1924, Elton had directed the institute into weaponising much of its research and opened the archives to EWE in return for continued control of the Institute as a semi-autonomous organisation. The most successful of Elton's directives had been the successful binding of barghests, entities that took the form of large hounds and formed the bases of myths in many cultures. The advisors assigned to EWE by both the Vatican and Anglican Church objected strongly on the grounds that creatures, in all probability, went beyond magic or even demonic. It was the view of both that the barghests were certainly Satanic in nature. The Reverend Robert Flower wrote to the Anglican Rites, Exorcisms and Banishments Committee (AREBaC) in May 1925 that:

> It is my view and that of many scholars that the hounds are from Him [Satan]. This has been born out by readings of the mythology of these islands as far back as 100 A.D. I draw you to the fact that they only manifested significantly following the Christianization of these Isles, surely as a counterpoint to the word of Christ, as recognized in the emergence of similar entities elsewhere. While we must harness all powers, holy, mystical and otherwise, for the greater good, we cannot allow Him in through any form.

AREBaC and its counterpart in the Vatican jointly condemned any attempts to use the barghests. EWE acquiesced to this request. Since its founding EWE had relied on the toleration, if not the support, of the main Christian Churches for its existence. A month after his first letter, Flower reported back to AREBaC that further development work on the utilization of barghests had ceased. It was true that development studies had ceased but Elton's intention had been to deploy a barghest operationally that November.

Taking place in remote parts of northern Iraq, trials commenced away from the prying eyes of AREBaC. Codenamed Operation Artemis, the trials used the creatures to hunt down insurgents and attack villages. During the following year, numerous so-called rebels and insurgents, counting civilians and children among their number, were located or exterminated through Artemis. In July 1928, its activities were extended to include trials in Palestine and India. Between November 1925 and April 1929, over 90% of targets assigned to Artemis units were successfully destroyed. The creatures left few tracks and had a tendency to almost entirely consume their prey. It seemed that the barghests were a viable mystical weapon.

While Artemis was proving the creatures capable of exterminating targets, concerning reports were emerging of regular rampages by them. Single target assassinations frequently turned into slaughters of anybody in the vicinity, including civilians and even Artemis personnel.

In September 1928, barghests on a tracking mission rampaged through a farm. All eight civilians present, as well as two of the creature's controllers, were killed, the attack officially being attributed to Kurdish militants. EWE had ordered an end to all operations to review procedures when, in February 1929, barghests turned on a newly established Artemis team in the Yukon. Eight of the twelve personnel were killed, while two more died of exposure due to the destruction of their camp. All of the Artemis teams were recalled, and further operations were suspended indefinitely.

The subsequent review of Operation Artemis concluded in 1931:

> It is estimated that of 60 targets designated across Iraq, Palestine, India and Ceylon, 55 were eliminated, alongside 200 additional persons. This number includes civilians and 20 EWE operatives. Loses amongst these operatives included highly skilled mystics drawn from across the Empire. Rampages have on occasion <u>commenced en route to operating areas</u> [underlining by author]. This risks compromising operations before they start, furthering the risk to EWE assets. In regard to the observations of James these theories are not substantiated and cannot be so. It is the recommendation of this committee that operations remain suspended until strategic necessity requires otherwise.

The final sentence was characteristic of EWE in the late inter-war period; a cautious approach that acknowledged both the inherent hazards of occult warfare and an appraisal of the worsening global political situation.

Although the committee's findings disappointed proponents of barghest operations, the reference to James reveals much about the focus of the committee. Roseanna James was a Jamaican mystic zoologist who had been approached by DExNA to study a clan of amphibious humanoids living in the Bayous of Louisiana. Impressed by her work, the Armitage Institute had engaged James to support Operation Artemis in Palestine, with the eventual aim of establishing a covert offshoot in the Yucatan.

The daughter of a pastor, James relished the opportunity to operate in the Holy Land. It was her Christian upbringing that led James to draw conclusions about the barghests. Independently of Flower and his recommendations to AREBaC, James concluded that there was what she described 'a higher malign power' behind the creatures. James further noted that while the figure of targets destroyed was in excess of 90%, this did not include aborted assignments. Almost exclusively, these aborted assignments occurred in the vicinity of holy sites. In such locations, the creatures either refused to appear or were unable to gain entry despite being in a spirit form. James believed that sites associated with the Abrahamic religions had the most significant impact on the capabilities of the barghests.

James gave lengthy testimony to the committee reviewing Artemis, but her evidence was not recorded in full. The committee derided James' opinion on the relationship between the barghests and Abrahamic religions, particularly Christianity. Records from pre-Christian times were evidence that creatures of similar nature existed across the world, while mystical practices in non-Christian cultures allowed their summoning. James had come before the committee to give evidence but increasingly felt the need to defend her reputation. Evidence from occultists who argued the creatures were all evolved from a single mystical species was dismissed.

It is likely that EWE could not countenance that the barghests were indeed satanic and that the advice of AREBaC should have been heeded. Whether as the result of arrogance, 'strategic necessity' or the malign influence identified by James, Artemis recommended in 1934 under the codenames Operation Cavall and Project Luison (the latter operating in Central America and the Caribbean). In broad terms, Cavall focused on potential frontline applications, while Luison evaluated counter-mystical operations and continued to assess the impact of religious sites on barghest operations. The latter proved particularly problematic and the Luison's mission was absorbed by Cavall in 1936, no solution having been found.

By 1939 British efforts to counter German occult offensives against Western Europe were focused on Operation Cavall, the support of vampires through the Taurus mission and research into counter spirit warfare. While the failure of Taurus had left a significant capability gap for Britain's own offensive capabilities in the occult field, they, unlike the French, had developed a range of countermeasures that were both active and passive. The British Expeditionary Force was supported by a number of counter-occult units. British covens had a history of volunteering their services to aid national defense, and the numbers doing so had grown in the 1930s. Their warding magics would play a crucial role throughout the war, protecting British and Allied forces across the globe. These covens and sabbats enjoyed a high degree of independence within British doctrine. They were provisionally under the ICG, which was itself part of EWE. The Northern Sabbat was particularly powerful. The Sabbat was fiercely independent and ruthlessly resisted attempts to absorb it. This led to some friction with EWE and APIB in particular. The mystics of the Northern Sabbat were held in high regard, and it maintained advisors assigned to, amongst others, the EOG, EWE, AREBaC and the Vatican.

Operation Tridamus was created in response to the terms of the Treaty of Carnac, a small but intensive effort by the British to maintain and develop a spirit warfare capability. By 1939, its primary operations had been a small number of assassinations of dissidents in the Empire and the summoning of pyrokinetic entities. These were likely demonic in origin and a blatant breach of the Treaty of Carnac. Only intensive warding efforts prevented their use from being revealed to the faes and a major diplomatic incident.

The strategy of *Guerre des Bêtes* was to be implemented through Cavall detachments, split between an expeditionary group in France and units in Britain. Those in Britain operated as part of EWE's General Defense Group. This included the ICG and occult formations such as Styx and, latterly, Nedu detachments. Styx detachments were tasked with countermeasures aimed at restricting enemy spirit operations through Hyperborean magic, sigils, runes and warding objects. The first Nedu detachment was created in July 1939 and immediately deployed to France. The group consisted primarily of Hindu mystics recruited from India, the codename related to a Sumerian deity being an effort to disguise this. The Nedu groups were created to actively counter enemy spirit forces by breaking binding rites and destroying them through various means. Nedu and Styx occupied an ambiguous position within the GDG. This was due to their being provisionally under the control of the Vortigern group, which was itself independent of EWE. This created some friction and a corresponding reduction in capability. The situation was to persist until 1943 when both were formerly absorbed into Vortigern.

On 1 September 1939, Nazi Germany launched its campaign against Poland. In support the Wehrmacht's Btl.SJ deployed two lycan companies that were tasked with locating and terminating Polish covens. Only one such coven was terminated, but two others were forced to relocate, creating a significant weakness in mystical defenses.

This should have enabled a number of spirit hosts to be summoned within and behind Polish lines. Instead, there were a number of small-scale raids that had little impact on the military situation beyond terrifying a handful of Polish soldiers.

On 5 October, Polish resistance ceased. During the campaign, the beasts of SS.Kp.K and the Wehrmacht's Btl.SJ had proved highly effective at tracking and engaging Polish occultists. This had enabled Germany's own covens and mystics to influence the battle. The expected *Geistkrieg* had not materialized despite extensive disruption of Polish defenses. This had been particularly apparent to the remote observers of the Ahnenerbe and Thule Society, who had monitored the ebb and flow of magical energies during the invasion.

Two days before the end of the Polish campaign Bilgic and Kellhof had been summoned to meet with senior Nazi mystics in Prague. The meeting had been called by those mystics, particularly those of the SS, Luftwaffe and Thule Society, who were hostile to *Geistkrieg* and preferred other modes of occult warfare. In particular, the Luftwaffe had argued for research to be focused on extradimensional entities, a view in part shared by the Thule Society.

The diaries of Ahnenerbe Colonel Gustav Honcher, present throughout, record a number of heated exchanges concerning the benefits or otherwise of Geistkrieg. It was the view of Honcher that:

At stake is nothing less than the direction of the mystical war effort. It seems clear to the mystics gathered here that while the Fuhrer's conventional military forces may match the British and French, in the mystical field, we face a tidal wave.

The reason for the failure of *Geistkrieg*, explained Kelhoff, was that the *Geist Korps* successfully trialed in Spain no longer existed. It had been torn apart and gutted by rival mystical organisations within Nazi Germany; its capabilities were shared piecemeal. The strategy lacked centralized direction and its power was diluted in such a way that summoning rites could easily nullified or swept away even by simple counter enchantments.

Kelhoff was supported in this view by Carla Deichmann of the Thule Society. An elementalist, Deichmann, had observed that spirit operations in Poland had only become of any significance with the capture of key natural sites. Background magic alone had, in fact, been able to counter German summoning efforts. Deichmann argued that the *Geist Korps* had succeeded as it was constituted of almost all of Germany's spirit-summoning mystics. These again needed to be centralized, providing a focus of power to both breach the defenses of their opponents and bind the most powerful spirits. It was an argument based on logic yet one that was anathema to organisations that were bitter rivals.

The result of the Prague Conference was a consolidation of sorts but largely within organisations. Kelhoff, disillusioned by the demise of the *Geist Korps*, became enthralled by the growing mystical abilities of the SS Granted the rank of major, Kelhoff would lead the first Wotan Detachment raised by the SS.[7] Bilgic had a disdain

---

[7] Wotan Detachments would gain a reputation for employing some of the most viscous and lethal spirits. On a number of occasion Wotan occult teams were wiped out in the field by the entities that they had summoned. It has been estimated that this accounted for 65% of losses suffered by the detachments from 1943.

for the racial policies of the SS and returned to Turkey, where she formed a group known as the Acolytes of Osiris. The Acolytes would bind a number of entities and were employed by the British, first in the Middle East and then the Horn of Africa, before eventually being recruited into the CBB for operations in Central Asia in 1945.

Formation	Location	Personnel
Warding and remote intelligence gathering		
Northern Sabbat	N. and E. England	13
Imperial Coven Group	Britain	?
Detachment 'Pendle'	France	4
Counter spirit warfare		
Styx Expeditionary Group	France	13
Styx General Defence Group	Southern England	9
Nedu Detachment 'Suvastu'	France	6
Counter IRA operations		
Cavall lycan Detachment Chulainn	Armagh	2
Seek and destroy operations		
Cavall Expeditionary Group	France	18
Cavall General Defence Group	Britain	
Operation Tridamus	Britain and France	8
Excalibur teams	France, Belgium, Netherlands	12
Counter spirit		
Vortigern	France/Britain	2 / 14

Figure 4: British occult formations available for duty on the Western Front, September 1939

Chapter 2

Hammer of a God

German occultists had demonstrated throughout the 1930s a capability to activate and, on occasion, utilise enchanted artefacts. In 1938, an Ahnenerbe team had retrieved one of the so-called Ry-lh tablets from beneath Angkor Wat in French Indo-China. They subsequently used inscriptions on the tablet to facilitate contact with an unknown entity. They then activated a second tablet in time to evade capture by a detachment of the French Foreign Legion using a teleportation spell. The Ankor Wat team had been fortunate as, from 1933, Excalibur operatives foiled a number of Nazi efforts to acquire artefacts. Sometimes, this was achieved through locating and seizing artefacts before the opposition could do so. Increasingly common from 1937 were confrontations between rival groups. All such operations were clandestine and occurred within even friendly countries without the knowledge of local authorities. It is estimated that twenty-four Excalibur agents lost their lives conducting such operations in the years from 1936 to 1939.

Countering Nazi efforts to acquire objects of occult significance relied upon effective intelligence. This was gathered from a variety of sources, both occult and conventional. By early 1940, it was rapidly becoming apparent to EWE's leadership that the Ahnenerbe had located a number of artefacts of potential war-winning power. The most concerning was intelligence received in January 1940 that the Nazis had reportedly located Mjolnir, the ancient hammer of Thor. It was a report that would send shockwaves through Allied occult agencies as the hammer's time in the materiel realm had been recorded as ending in the late seventh century by the Norse alchemist Gurnssen. Evidently archaeologists at the University of Copenhagen had acquired the hammer from a meteor impact crater in Greenland during an expedition of 1921. The hammer may have lay in a storeroom unnoticed had it not been for one Helmut Klenz.

Klenz had been a junior archaeologist in the expedition of 1921 and later a committed Nazi, an advisor on Scandinavian folklore to both the Ahnenerbe and Black Sun organisation. In March 1938, while sifting through the archives of the University of Oslo on unrelated matters, Klenz stumbled upon a description of Mjolnir recorded by Gurnssen. His sharp mind instantly made the connection between this and the seemingly anomalous object recovered in 1921. It was clear to Klenz that he could deliver to his Nazi masters in Berlin not only the weapon of a God but one of no less than a Norse deity.

Klenz covertly removed the text containing the description and headed straight for the German embassy, knowing that the Kriegsmarine intelligence service had recently assigned a scrying team to the naval attaché in Oslo. The team was led by Otto Baylerlain, a one-time sceptic who had been converted following a near-deadly encounter with an entity in Cologne in 1936. As was often the case with the occult detachments operated by the Kriegsmarine at this stage of the conflict, the results of the scrying were somewhat vague and inconsistent. Only in 1942 would the Germans perfect the manufacture of mirrors of correct purity for accurate scrying. Bayerlain's team were nonetheless able to confirm during the course of multiple attempts that Mjolnir was indeed still in storage beneath the University of

Copenhagen. It also appeared that there were potential artefacts of similar or greater power stored there. While this may have been the case in 1938, by 1940, EWE's own psychic efforts did not detect such additional artefacts. Post-war analysis of the archives supported this conclusion.

What had caused Bayerlain to so dramatically misinterpret the situation has been the subject of some debate in occult circles ever since. The trend was for Nazi scrying efforts at this time to underestimate or miss facts outright. To greatly overestimate in this way was nearly unknown until much later in the war, when the Ahnenerbe and others began to experiment with chemical and even genetic enhancement of its scrying and psychic intelligence gathering teams. It may have been that the resonance of the hammer itself had disrupted the scrying effort, but no similar effect had been experienced by the British team in 1940, and this would surely have been the case, even if their superior capabilities were considered. It was the opinion of Roy McKay, a senior archaeologist on the EWE team, that the interference was caused by none other than the Norse God Loki. This was certainly not the only time that Loki's influence would be felt in occult activities during the war years. Yet his motives, if any did exist, are as ever hard to understand.

If Loki had indeed interfered with the intention of motivating Klenz it had been a great success. Klenz immediately set off for Berlin via boat to Hamburg, no doubt formulating a plan for the retrieval, activation and use of Mjolnir to further the Nazis' cause. On 12th April 1938, Klenz presented his proposal to Himmler and Hitler's astrologer. Like Klenz, the military mind of Himmler saw the opportunity presented by gaining control of an object of such power but it was the thought of the near ethnic purity of its Norse origins that attracted him the most. What better than the opportunity to wield the power of an Aryan God to crush the Slavs and any opponents in the Reich?

It is almost certain that plans were made at the meeting for Mjolnir to be acquired. Within days, orders were drawn up for the German embassy to make enquiries about a certain object of cultural significance to be purchased from the University of Copenhagen. Klenz was to travel to the city on 17th April to oversee the purchase. A cruel act of irony, or perhaps divine intervention, occurred on the 16th of April. Klenz's car was found inexplicably burned out on the road to the airport, his charred remains found inside, and his papers reduced to ash. No explanation could be found, although a post war investigation of Ahnenerbe archives would reveal that local people reported a lightning bolt that morning, a lightning bolt from an otherwise clear sky. Whether this was a coincidence, divine intervention or a freak accident is impossible to determine.

Perhaps distracted by gathering war clouds in Europe or possibly wary of Klenz's fate, Himmler made no further plans to purchase Mjolnir. Indeed, the hammer seems to have been forgotten until plans began to be made in 1939 for a German assault on Scandinavia. The existence of Mjolnir may have been shared by senior Nazis during a meeting with the pro-Nazi Norwegian defense minister Vidkun Quisling in December of that year. What better way for the Nazis and their Norwegian puppets to bring Norway to heal than with the power of Thor's Hammer? It may be that Quisling envisaged himself leading a country transformed into some earthly Valhala for he certainly embraced the support of the Nazis, leading a puppet government after their occupation of his country in April 1940.

Whatever the intended outcomes, this time there would be no need to purchase the object as it could be taken by force. Denmark and thus Copenhagen were to be a stepping stone in the German invasion of Norway. The operation intended to secure the hammer was codenamed Sturmschild and was to have been a combination of simplicity and outright audacity. A force of sixteen elite and heavily armed Brandenburger soldiers would be smuggled into Copenhagen aboard a coal transport, travel to the university from the harbour on the morning of the invasion in cars arranged by the embassy, secure Mjolnir and hold out until relieved by invading forces. It was expected that Danish forces would be too concerned with the actual invasion to notice, let alone respond, to a raid at a university. It was the simplicity of this plan that would result in the eventual retrieval of the hammer by the British.

At this early stage of the war, elements of the Abwehr had been giving both active and passive support to the British. Infiltration of the organisation had been enhanced through the vetting of potential contacts psychically by G Office operatives and the allies' tentative first steps in psychic manipulation. One such Abwehr officer, who had proved particularly vulnerable to manipulation, noticed the unusual interest of the Brandenburgers in the seemingly unimportant university archive. Further investigation revealed links to the meeting of April 1938. EWE's attention was gained, and their own scrying was initiated. It was clear that Klenz had been onto something war-changing, if not outright war-winning, and just as Himmler recognized, control of Mjolnir had potential implications for political control of Scandinavia and the whole ideology of an Aryan super race. British fears of German ascendency in Scandinavia threatened to become a reality.

EWE had already been focusing the attention of its B Office on Denmark after German efforts to psychically influence Danish commanders and political leaders had been detected. The result was that a coven of East Anglian witches had been casting disruptive spells and wards since December 1939 in an attempt to limit the impact of the Abwher's influence on Danish decision-makers. It was apparent that more direct action would be needed and that this action would need to take place rapidly least, German invasion plans would be implemented before Mjolnir could be recovered.

A pre-emptive military expedition against Copenhagen was out of the question. Denmark was too close to Germany to take such a risk and it was considered that Anglo-French forces would be at full stretch attempting to secure Norway to undertake meaning full activity in Denmark. Military realities aside, the political consequences of such an intervention were unacceptable, particularly as it appeared a number of key leaders in Denmark had fallen victim to German psychic efforts. Mjolnir would need to be acquired through less drastic means. Fortunately for the allies they already had an asset active in the area who possessed the skills required for the task. He was Lieutenant Michael Wishard.

Wishard was an Excalibur agent assigned to the Baltic region as part of Operation Tidal Wave. This had commenced in 1936 to spearhead Anglo-French diplomatic initiatives aimed at cooperation with the various species of Merfolk that resided in Northern European waters. Wishard had knowledge of the creatures after encountering them while lost overboard during a naval exercise in the North Sea in 1932, during which time he survived thanks to assistance from Merfolk, who dwelled off the coast of Norway. By 1939, Wishard had learned the language of the tribe in question and privately funded his own expedition to make contact again. Wishard's cold, calculating personality was a perfect fit for the ocean dwellers and he had rapidly been befriended by the tribe.

By 1940, further links had been established with other tribes of that particular Mer species throughout the Skagerrak. On 3 January 1940, Wishard was led to the court of the tribe's chieftain, at which he was able to discuss the politics of the surface world. Initially the Mer chieftain had sought a policy of neutrality following the offer of a trade deal with the Reich by visiting SS delegation Lurwitz. The goodwill towards the Nazis soon evaporated: operatives of the Kriegsmarine's Ozean-Abteilung Krake (O.Abt.K) had been discovered attempting to abduct a serpent from the Royal menagerie. This effort to bolster German naval strength in the North Sea had misfired dramatically.

While the serpent had made a meal of the O.Abt.K team, Merfolk's retaliation was swift and brutal. That same night, the SS delegation was offered as a sacrifice to Posdon the Seedrache; a number of German vessels would be lost in unexplained circumstances during the following months, while French observers assigned to the Mers would later attest to the savagery shown towards German sailors found a drift in the seas following naval battles around Norway. German incompetence had, not for the final time, handed the allies the opportunity for an alliance with a mystic race. The opportunity was not squandered, and a treaty was formally signed aboard a British warship in January 1940. Finally, Wishard's work with the Merfolk was at a stage in which field trials of human–Mer cooperation could begin.

Region	Declared allegiance			
	Allied	Axis	USSR	Confirmed neutrality
Baltic	1	1	0	0
North Sea	1	1	0	1
Barents & Norwegian Seas	1	0	1	0
Arctic Ocean	1	0	0	1
North Atlantic Ocean (British Isles)	2	1	0	0
North Atlantic Ocean (European coast)	1	0	0	0

Figure 5: The diplomatic allegiances of the Mer Tribes, September 1939

The way was now open for Mjolnir to be retrieved from Copenhagen. Based in the city, Wishard had regular contact with the anthropology department of the university and was able to quickly locate the precise whereabouts of the hammer. Aided by deception spells, this was achieved without the knowledge of the Ahnenerbe operatives monitoring the University. Two days after receiving authorization, and only hours before Sturmschild was enacted, Wishard removed Mjolnir from the university and headed to the harbor. The irony was that he was likely only meters from the coal freighter being used as the base for German operation and its team of Brandenburgers while driving into the harbor to rendezvous with his Merfolk support team.

The rendezvous would have passed without any problems had it not been for an intervention by two members of O.Abt.K. The department had been monitoring Merfolk's activity. Wary of British interest and SS incompetence, O.Abt.K had ordered its own team into Copenhagen.

What happened next is confusing. Based on British reports, the German team opened fire, causing Wishard to dive for cover with the artefact. As per the Bermuda Treaty, Wishard ordered his Merfolk operatives not to engage humans directly, resulting in one of the three being injured. The British agents then returned fire. The Germans were quickly felled in the fusillade, and bodies and cars were dumped into the harbor. The records of the Copenhagen police contain a different version of events. Soon after midnight, a near hysterical fisherman staggered into a nearby police station, reporting how green 'fish monsters' had pounced upon two unfortunates in the harbor. They removed the head of one person 'as if unscrewing a jam jar' and dragged the remains of both into the sea.

Records captured by DExNA after the war confirm the loss of a two-man O.Abt.K team on that night after being sent 'to interdict' a suspected joint Allied-Merfolk operation. Perhaps Wishard had followed procedure and the protocols of the Bermuda Treaty, although this would have been one of the rare times in which operatives from any side obeyed them after 1939. If he had followed them, maybe the Merfolk would have removed the bodies to the sea. The Copenhagen police certainly reported nothing else in relation to the case, but within hours their country would be occupied and further investigation halted by the invasion. Whatever happened in the final hours before the occupation of Denmark by German forces, Mjolnir was delivered by a British submarine to a Norwegian naval vessel in the North Sea. Not for the last time during the war, the arrival of a British submarine close to enemy waters would be facilitated by Merfolk's efforts to disable enemy sea mines.

With perhaps the greatest weapon in Scandinavian history secure, the way was set for Norway to resist the

Nazis' occupation. While the Norwegians would evacuate a number of artefacts to safety, including a throne once used by Odin, it was Mjolnir who was the prize Himmler had sought. The hammer initially remained in storage in Britain, protected by anti-divination wards. In August 1943, the SOE's Apollo Section, the so-called Occult Operations Executive (OOE) but officially designated SOEAS, used information from a Templar Shrine in Syria to begin activating the hammer. This was undertaken as part of Project Trebuchet.[8] The result was that by 1945, limited testing of the Hammer's properties was underway in Iceland. Norwegians embedded within Emerald, the French Navy's Occult Combat Unit, submitted plans to use the power of Mjolnir in the event of an Allied invasion of Norway in 1945.

It was known that the Germans had constructed significant underground facilities in Norway. Protected by unusually strong wards and other remote sensing defences. It was feared that the Nazis would amass significant conventional and occult forces for a final last stand. Every means employed to infiltrate the bases failed, and this constituted the most complete counter-intelligence and counter-warding operation conducted by the Germans throughout the war. To the allies, it was unclear whether this was merely a successful effort or something far more sinister: was what was contained within the bunkers themselves so powerful as to prevent disclosure by remote sensing means?

The Nazis had indeed been busy in Norway. As early as 1940 two covens from eastern Germany had been sent to counter Allied efforts to collect intelligence through occult

---

[8] See Chapter 6 'Project Trebuchet'

means. This was bolstered by the deployment in 1942 of a cryptid platoon and a section of Carpathian Werebeasts. With defeat in sight, Nazi efforts to fortify Norway for the final apocalyptic battle in Aryan lands gathered pace. Deployments from the Kriegsmarine in Spring 1945 included not only the latest U-boats but also a platoon of Mer-beings, two seedrache and several O.Abt.K teams accompanied by equipment derived from Atlantaen sources. Two war saucers arrived in late March from SS testing grounds, joined by a squadron of Me262Z fighters. Lycan Companies provided security. The source of the interference of Allied remote sensing activities was discovered to have been an improved prototype of the rift-generating device utilised on the Luftwaffe's own Die Glocke. This had been deployed in an effort to set up an ether transfer bridge linking the Norwegian bunkers to Berlin in the event of complete Allied encirclement.

Backed by such technology, the conventional forces of the Reich could have held out for months or years in a fanatical last stand. Two bunker complexes even included experimental hydroponic farms, with energy for desalinization and heating provided by the Die Glocke prototype. It was thus fortunate that it was decided to conduct a demonstration of the Mjolnir's power within the borders of Germany. The location selected was Thuringia in Germany, and in the closing weeks of the war, a number of German officials and leading occultists were invited to observe the test. The strike on German soil, conducted from a weapon held underground in Iceland, had the desired effect. Nazis' plans for a last stand in Norway were dropped.

With no last stand to fight in Norway, Mjolnir was placed in deep storage on an island above the Arctic Circle. Those knowledgeable of the occult within the Allied military had been impressed by the results of the Thuringia test. It was thus proposed to use the hammer as a covert backup in case the Manhattan Project had failed. What better way to hide the employment of a mystical weapon, it was reasoned, than with a supposed marvel of the modern age? Ultimately the atomic bomb proved useable and fully understood by scientists. Thus, interest in the hammer waned. The fate of the hammer after the war remains a closely guarded secret. Rumors persist that it was amongst a number of artefacts traded with Aldebaran delegates during the Sahara Accords of 1974.

Chapter 3

Geistkrieg

The period of the Phony War was characterized by efforts to ensure that occult operations were kept from public view. It was clear that The Bermuda Treaty could no longer prevent bloodshed, but all occultists remained wary of a backlash from the general populace and a return to the persecution of magic users. Hence, such forces continued to be used for espionage, reconnaissance, harassment, and to counter similar enemy operations. Sightings of spirits, Lycans and other creatures were frequently classified as the result of hallucinations caused by combat fatigue, insanity or exhaustion. During the Norwegian campaign, a number of German military personnel were executed by SS.Kp.K. to limit 'the spread of dangerous rumors'. A similar role was adopted by British Cavall units in June 1940. It was a pattern that would continue to varying intensities throughout the war.[9]

Espionage operations against Germany and 'allies' alike formed the core commitment of the Excalibur teams deployed to the continent. Following the fall of Poland, Excalibur operatives from R Office were particularly active across Western Europe. Particularly important was locating and assessing artefacts held in both national archives and private collections. When Fall Gelb, the German offensive in the West, commenced on 10 May 1940, Excalibur

---

[9] The number of operational security missions of this nature remain classified due to ongoing operations and the development of continuing capabilities.

operatives conducted a number of operations to secure such artefacts. In Ghent, an Excalibur agent had covertly infiltrated the staff of an archanist known to have fascist sympathies. A number of manuscripts belonging to the civilization of Mu were discovered, and the remainder were destroyed to prevent their capture by the Nazis. The agent made good his escape and managed to kill two pursuing Ahnenerbe operatives.

Less successful was an Excalibur operation on 11 May aimed at securing Ry-lh artefacts from the Belgian government's Black Archive. The convoy was ambushed by lycans of the Wehrmacht's Btl.SJ, resulting in the deaths of all four operatives and the loss of the artefacts. Operations in the Netherlands were fully supported by the Dutch Navy's Afdeling voor Uitgebreide Oorlogsvoering (Department for Extended Warfare) or AUO. The Dutch-led evacuation of artefacts, codenamed Operation Ossaert, had been initiated on 9 May, and the operation ended in the early hours of 14 May, one day before the Dutch surrender. Ossaert had been a near complete success and deprived Nazi mystics of a number of Zarlin artefacts retrieved by the Dutch from the Dutch East Indies, the remains of a Nephilim and wreckage of a spacecraft that had crashed in the Zuiderzee in 1932. The latter would provide key technology for the US Navy's experiments with invisibility in 1943.

The initial Excalibur operations in response to the German invasion of the Low Countries deprived the Nazis of objects that would have been of considerable value to their war effort. Interrogated by Sapphire operatives in 1948, Ahnenerbe Scientist Friedrich Halst stated:

Black Sun contented themselves with the technologies that we gained from the extra-terrestrials through the Aaland Treaty. But Die Glocke and the K'lmar technologies were just toys compared to what the Dutch retrieved. If they could have activated the reactor even in its damaged state, it could have outperformed our later Haunebu designs... It is my view that magic was obsolete compared to technology by then [1943], but Zarlin mystics could summon entities of a power that our geist-mancers could only dream of. Who knows what we could have achieved with even a fraction of what the Dutch had acquired.

Despite these early successes for the Allies' occult forces, there were causes for concern. Co-operation between British and French occultists had been ineffective. On 12 May, an operation to escort a fae delegation from southern Belgium was intercepted by entities summoned by SS Woden Detachment Pluto. The escorting Excalibur team was wiped out and was due to have been supported by lycan's of France's UAMS 'Languedoc'. The lycan's deployed in accordance with Saphhire's 'seek and destroy doctrine' while Excalibur tended to operate in close coordination with their own such units.

Failures of cooperation were almost inevitable, given the history of mistrust between Anglo-French forces. More concerning for EWE was the unexpected effectiveness of German spirit warfare. The ineffectiveness of this form of warfare in Poland had been misinterpreted by EWE as evidence of an overestimation of German capabilities in this field and the efficiency of mystical countermeasures. Such was EWE's confidence that most of the Nedu and Styx teams had been withdrawn from France that March. Now, with the threat of German spirit forces becoming apparent, counter operations were being conducted by the four strong 'Pendle Detachment'. This overstretched Pendle as it was primarily tasked with remote viewing operations and had only limited capabilities to effectively counter spirits. French capabilities were more significant but spread along a much wider front and relied on UAMS to track down and terminate groups of enemy mystics who were involved in summoning.

Weak Allied countermeasures enabled German Geist formations to operate both on and behind the frontlines. Particularly devastating was the German strategy of Geistergeschütze (ghost ordnance). This took advantage of the non-corporeal nature of spirits. Specifically, this enabled them to operate within artillery fire zones, using their capabilities to add to the devastation or conduct reconnaissance while under bombardment within British and French formations. On 13 May, spirits of the Abwehr's 'Gruppe Lindwurm' infiltrated deep into the French lines, pinpointing the location of a number of UAMS units. It was an opportunity that the Ahnenerbe had long planned for.

In 1938 Ahnenerbe operatives had become aware of both the French UAMS and British Cavall formations. The result was Silberscherbe des Kriegsplans (War Plan Silver Shard). As early as 1934, the Wehrmacht, Luftwaffe and Ahnenerbe had all independently conducted experiments to test the vulnerability of Lycans to larger calibre modern weaponry. It was found that the vulnerability was such that all lycan units would only be marginally more survivable than human ones on the modern battlefield. While the Wehrmacht and Luftwaffe both decided to limit the role of lycans to covert operations, the Ahnenerbe recognized that countermeasures may still be needed if lycans were to become a significant force in the armies of foreign or domestic opponents. It was the latter, particularly in regard to the SA and Wehrmacht, which caused the most concern in the higher echelons of the Ahnenerbe. Such was competition within the Third Reich there was even a fear that if loyalties collapsed within the SS, Ahnenerbe operatives would lack the firepower to fight their former colleagues. Silver Shard was a consequence of studies preparing for such a possible civil war within Germany.

From 1936, Ahnenerbe operatives, aided by supporters within the Thule Society, were able to secretly infiltrate German munitions factories. Focusing principally on those factories producing artillery shells, quantities of silver were added to shell casings. The result was that an estimated 20 to 35% of artillery rounds available on the frontline contained sufficient silver to trigger an anaphylactic reaction within lycans, in addition to the effect of high explosives. Through Silver Shard, approximately 8% of bombs available to the Luftwaffe contained similar quantities of silver. While the leadership of the Ahnenerbe did not trust their military colleagues within the SS, they were able to use their influence to ensure units near the frontline were stocked with Silver Shard munitions. Using the pretext of information 'gained through mystical means,' the Ahnenerbe directed an intensive bombardment against the UAMS. Laced with silver that was effectively toxic to their lycan forces, the effects were devastating. At a stroke, the Ahnenerbe had not only field-tested a counter to potential rivals in Germany but also crippled the keystone of French active countermeasures against occult forces.

Silver Shard would eventually become known to the wider Nazi establishment in 1944, when its existence was deliberately leaked by occultists within the Abwehr to discredit opponents. The SS leadership was incensed that elements within its own organisation had made plans to fight SS forces, leading to a number of bloody purges. As late as 5 May 1945, SS soldiers were still being tasked with destroying stockpiles of suspected Silver Shard shells even as the Third Reich collapsed. Ironically, EWE had become aware of Silver Shard in 1941. In cooperation with the SOE's Apollo section, they would actively add silver to German heavy munitions production in preparation for a potential civil war fought by lycans within Germany.

The devastation suffered by the UAMS would be swiftly followed up by the beasts of SS.Kp.K and the Wehrmacht's Btl. SJ. Lycans within these forces suffered heavily from silver contamination within the bombardment zones, and a number of clashes reportedly occurred between these supposedly allied formations. However, by the dawn of 15 May, 70% of the UAMS' effective strength had ceased to exist, leaving Anglo-French counter-mystical forces in disarray and unable to significantly influence the tide of the battle. The Thule Society's Hexenzirkel Witzel (Coven Witzel) took advantage of this to cast a number of deception enchantments, preventing French deployments against German breakthroughs in critical areas of northern France. A further German success was achieved on 21 May when a Nedu detachment en route to the headquarters of the B.E.F. was ambushed by a detachment of Wehrmacht lycans.

Any hope of retrieving the deteriorating Anglo-French military situation through mystical means effectively ended on 25 May. On the day of the Belgian collapse, British, French and U.S. military missions (the latter acting as observers) were summoned to the high council of the Northern French fae kingdoms at Soissons. EWE had long been angered by fae intransigence against the Germans, but now the fae announced their neutrality in what they deemed to be a war between mortals. Kelvin Roberts was a Rhodesian in the British mission and wrote that:

> There was disbelief at the fae's decision. The threat posed by the Nazis was clearly evident from the experience of faes in Germany, Spain [during and after the civil war], Poland and now Western Europe itself. The worst part was the sense of betrayal. The fae of France had been tardy allies but at least there had been the promise of support. Worse was that at Carnac we had bargained away valuable military capabilities [in regard to spirit warfare] in return for support that was never delivered. It is my belief that it was never intended to be so.

The perceived betrayal of the fae would have a profound impact on subsequent French occult warfare, with mysticism taking a much-reduced role within Free French doctrine. There were elements that called for a military response. The 3rd UAMS was redeployed from the Italian frontier two days later and deployed to Brittany, the heart of fae power within continental Western Europe. 3rd UAMS was later joined by members of the Templar Sect known as 'The Hammer of Cain' who had enlisted in the French army en masse in 1939. Days later, French occult forces began reprisals against their former fae allies. In early July 1940, soon after the fall of France, teams from the Thule Society attempted to contact a number of fae leaders but reported scenes of devastation and carnage in their settlements. It is believed that fae populations in the region were reduced to 15% of their pre-war levels by 1946.

It was clear to the British that they were facing a crisis in their occult strategy. There was a need to evacuate the BEF, while opponents of EWE within the British establishment were certain to use its recent failures to seize some of its power. On 22 May, Operation Tridamus was ordered by EWE to 'use all means at your disposal to safeguard the evacuation of British forces. Carnac is now dead. Proceed as you wish. The last sentence was aimed directly at the commander of Tridamus, Robert Flynn-Gaunt.

Appointed at the time of the project's creation in 1938, Flynn-Gaunt was a vocal opponent of the terms within the Carnac Treaty that limited British development of spirit warfare capability. It was a view shared with EWE's leadership, who fully anticipated Flynn-Gaunt would take action to circumvent the treaty without overtly breaking in. As a demonologist schooled in both Western Chinese and sub-Saharan magics, Flynn-Gaunt recruited mystics from across the globe with the aim of summoning and binding a number of entities. It was rumored that the most powerful entity within the power of Tridamus was Adrammelech of Samaria, while there were also a number of extra-terrestrial entities originating from systems in the vicinity of Aldebaran. It was later theorised that the activities of Tridamus had come to the attention of the fae and had contributed to their decision to withdraw from their obligations.

In December 1939, Tridamus planners had developed a strategy to be implemented if there was a need to rapidly secure an area to support British operations. Codenamed Pantheon, it seemed to offer a solution to the defense of the Dunkirk perimeter against German occult forces. It was a plan that sought to integrate both the lesser spirits and more powerful entities that could be commanded by Tridamus.

France's Onyx organisation was particularly critical of a plan that sought to unleash such entities on French territory. Such was their concern that on 27 December 1940, delegates from Onyx and Sapphire met at Marseille to discuss contingencies should the binding rituals for Pantheon prove ineffective.

Flynn-Gaunt ruthlessly dismissed French fears. Consequentially, Pantheon was a solely British operation. Even the Dutch AUO and a recently arrived Polish coven refused to participate. Even Britain's EOG was skeptical and released only one coven to support the operation. Flynn-Gaunt was undeterred and proceeded to exploit his mystics to bind a host of powerful entities around the Dunkirk perimeter. The strength of the enchantments (including hiding the entities from human eyes) required the participation of ICG covens in both France and Southern England. Many of the entities had to be held in place by complex runes and sigils. On 24 May, Flynn-Gaunt reported to his superiors:

> It pleases me to report to their Lordships that the perimeter of the evacuation zone and the area contained within it are immune to attack by enemy magical and supernatural elements. As per directives the deployment is to be covert so as to prevent panic amongst conventional formations. The demands on the focus of the covens binding and shrouding the entities are such that I anticipate the cordon enduring a little more than seven days so we must act swiftly.

The inherent dangers of the plan became apparent on 25 May when 30% of occultists assigned to the summoning and binding were rendered inoperative, many fatally. The allocation of ICG assets from northern France also weakened counter-enchantment capabilities at a time when the German attack continued to gain momentum. SS.Kp.K and the Luftwaffe's NZL ruthlessly exploited this to locate and destroy a number of Sapphire's remaining covens and mystics. Geist units of the Wehrmacht were simultaneously deployed to disrupt French operations by removing road signs and interfering with attempts to destroy bridges and other installations.

Despite the opportunities taken to continue the pursuit of French forces, it was rapidly becoming apparent to the Germans that something was amiss in the British sector. Seers and remote viewers reported an inability to penetrate the area, and those of Gruppe Lindwurm reported fatal counterattacks across the astral plain by 'unknown beings of demonic origin'. Geist units were simply torn to pieces or vigorously resisted summoning.[10] The latter was not unusual but made easier for spirits by the disruptive presence of the entities summoned by Pantheon. An effort to launch an assault on the eastern perimeter of Dunkirk on the night of 25 May resulted in the destruction of a number of lycans and other beasts, including several recently summoned Draugr. An urgent conference between the Ahnenerbe, Thule Society and others was convened. Colonel Gustav Honcher attended as an advisor to the Ahnenerbe on field operations. He recorded in his diary:

> For the first time, there was terror amongst the gathered leaders of German military mysticism. Major Anders looked deathly grey; his daughter was in a coven assigned north of the Somme. Rosenburg

---

[10] As a mystic assigned to Gruppe Lindwurm grimly noted 'when the dead fear to tread, it is folly to continue'.

of the Thule [Society] drank endlessly. At Prague [in October 1939], the fear had been of failure, but this was much more. It was the fear of the unknown, a fear of what unearthly power the enemy had summoned. Abwehr remote viewers had been slain on the astral plane. Entities claiming to be Wendigos, Oni and ifrit were among the devils and demons reported. Seers as far away as Warsaw had been driven mad by dark whispers. The Thule Society feared such a host could only be summoned by a dark pact or worse; the British could not control what they had brought forth. Black Sun psychics reported extra-terrestrial beings alongside a devil. What did the British intend next with such a host?[11]

The delegates concluded that not only were continued occult operations against Dunkirk impossible but that, in desperation, the British may have been ready to unleash demonic forces in defence. For their part, the Ahnenerbe and Thule Society could offer no defence. Hitler's infamous halt order, Adrammelech of Samaria, was thus issued to the panzers on 26 May.

As Germany's occultists prepared for the British to unleash Hell on Earth, the British themselves were experiencing difficulties. By 28 May British covens were exhausted by the exertion of maintaining the Pantheon entities. Far from a little over seven days' boasted by Flynn-Gaunt, the entities had remained for barely four. An attempt by the Northern Sabbat to maintain a ruse of simulated entity activity failed, and the German halt order Adrammelech of Samaria was rescinded. The exertion of creating, binding

---

[11] Information in brackets added by the author.

and maintaining the Pantheon entities had cost the lives of many British mystics and depowered others, some until after the war ended. Pantheon had lasted only half of the promised duration. Nevertheless, considerable damage had also been inflicted on the German spirit and lycan forces in the opening phases. Importantly, it had also gave the British time to evacuate through the lull created by the halt order.

There was to be a further, far-reaching consequence of the operation. It was now clear to both sides that the large-scale employment of entities was not feasible, while the demands or even a small-scale demonic binding could be costly. AREBaC had been outraged, seeing Pantheon as being one step removed from working with Satan. They threatened to withdraw support from EWE and other organisations. No operation on the scale of Pantheon was repeated by any nation. The British, however, had gained an interest in demonic warfare. On 3 June, Flynn-Gaunt had left Dunkirk with a new directive from EWE: to prepare Operation Tridamus for the defense of Britain.

By 4 June, the British had evacuated Dunkirk, and the German pursuit of the French continued. By this time, the only significant concentration of French occult capability was that of operating alongside the 4th Army. This offered the force some protection from harassment by German forces, and it was able to launch a number of counterattacks, albeit unsuccessfully. By this stage of the campaign, rapid advances made spell casting and enchantments difficult, while the fluid nature of the front lines rendered remote viewing of tactical objectives impractical. On 21 June, France surrendered, and its occult forces relocated to Africa through Operation Blood Raven.[12]

---

[12] See Chapter 8 'Marine Leviathans'

Chapter 4

Operation Charon

During the 1930s EWE's activities had increasingly focused on events occurring overseas. Operations within the British Isles were primarily directed by H Office but many of its assets, including a number of Excalibur agents, had been assigned to other departments. The result was that EWE's domestic operation relied on MI5's Guinevere group, which itself was under-resourced. EWE, like many elements of the British establishment, had not anticipated the collapse of Anglo-French resistance in 1940. Thus, there was alarm at the limited capability available to counter the type of occult operations that were expected to occur before, during and after an invasion of Britain.

Since September 1939, EWE had been able to 'encourage' a significant number of occultists to act through patriotism, blackmail or intimidation. By the summer of 1940, as the Battle of Britain raged in the skies of Southern England, this source of recruitment had been drastically reduced. The numbers of potential recruits were limited, and many found themselves recruited by other agencies, including those of foreign powers. This included Sapphire, DExNA, the AUO and the CBB. It was not unusual for even the organisations of 'minor nations' such as Spain to attract such occultists.

On 1 July 1940, the following instructions were sent by EWE to diplomatic missions assigned to Britain's fae kingdoms.

Missions are to approach fae leaders directly with the objective of securing personnel of fae origin. These fae are to be recruited directly into our forces. It is certain that the long-standing ties between our cultures and a common enemy will ease this endeavor.

This appraisal of British-fae relations proved to be grossly optimistic and was very much symptomatic of the arrogance displayed by EWE's leadership towards the fae.

Ties with the Mer tribes around Britain had been nurtured through Operation Tidal Wave; policy towards the land-based fae had been to presume that they would fall into line against a common enemy. The problem for the British was that the fae had started to question just who the enemy was. A number of fae nobles had been killed in suspicious circumstances in the proceeding decade, and the fae suspected a covert programme of assassination orchestrated by AREBaC and the Vatican.[13] Britain's fae's felt betrayed by the actions carried out under Operation Tridamus in the defense of Dunkirk. The fae knew too well the dangers posed by such reckless summoning and increasingly viewed EWE activities with suspicion.

A Grand Moot of all fae kingdoms was called at Winchester on 5 July. Its decision was not unanimous but a declaration was made to the effect that co-operation would only occur between Britain and the fae if it was directly in the interests of the latter to do so. That divisions existed within the fae kingdoms was acknowledged in that each lord

---

[13] This was partly true. AREBaC had acted in conjunction with Nimue against fae deemed 'likely to under the sway of Satan'. Operations of this nature continued into the 1980s.

was encouraged to act according to their own interests while acknowledging the guidance of the declaration. It was made clear that any German attack on fae sacred sites would be considered an act of war against all British fae.

EWE welcomed the final fae declaration but it was as much aimed at the Germans as the British. Many fae lords maintained diplomatic contacts with the Nazis through the Ahnenerbe, Thule Society and Black Sun organisations. It was likely they felt that this would be enough to deter aggression in the event of a German invasion. No doubt of greater comfort to Germany was that, in the short term at least, cooperation between the British and Fae would remain limited. A faction of pro-British fae lords formed around Nimue but EWE estimated almost 80% were neutral or outright hostile.[14] Worse was to follow when a number of fae lords who were eager to show their neutrality elected to temporarily disenchant certain sacred sites within their realms. Desperate for mystics and with access to sacred sites limited during a time of crisis, EWE was running out of options.

Despite its short duration and damage inflicted on British forces, Operation Pantheon had highlighted the possibility of utilising entities of even greater power. Since returning from Dunkirk Flynn-Gaunt had been working alongside the Armitage Institute to identify the most powerful entities that could be bound. Elton retained leadership of the institute, having been promoted to Wing Commander and effectively made second in command of APIB. Elton proposed going one step further than Flynn-Gaunt, Britain, he argued, faced an existential crisis, so if the

---

[14] The kingdoms of northern England and Wales were seen as particularly suspect.

most powerful entities could not be bound through conventional occult practise, why not get their support through other means? Or, as Elton wrote to Flynn-Gaunt that July, 'get them to do the job now and pay their bill later'.

EWE's leadership was wary of repeating Pantheon. The operation had caused considerable damage to Britain's occult capabilities and operations had been curtailed. This included an expedition to find the lost city of the Ysa Gon civilization in Afghanistan, the city being shielded by powerful warding spells. Ironically, an operation such as Pantheon, albeit repeated on a much smaller scale, offered the possibility of rectifying the reduction in Britain's mystical capabilities that the initial operation had caused.

AREBaC was outraged at the suggestion that Pantheon was to be repeated in any form. A strongly worded statement, addressed to EWE and APIB, was issued by AREBaC's central committee on 13 July:

> It is impossible for us to sanction any attempt at doing business with such entities. Any such operation would, by necessity, result in the immediate withdrawal of all cooperation with EWE and the withdrawal of all AREBaC assets from ongoing operations. We would have no choice but to consider any party consorting with such entities, be it EWE, APIB, ICG or otherwise, to be a potential threat to stability in the occult sphere.

Adam Johnson was the senior British Army Chaplain assigned to AREBaC. He wrote to Colonel George Sanders, his superior at the British Army's Esoteric Operations Group, on 22 July the leadership [of AREBaC] is incensed at the proposal originating from the Armitage Institute. Events in France [Pantheon] has stretched patience to the limit and I very much fear a fracturing of relations is inevitable. The points raised are valid and I feel that as a man of God I too would act accordingly with my beliefs.

Johnson was later called before AREBaC's central committee and instructed to explore the possibility of raising 'a small body of devout men for operations to further the mission of AREBaC'. The organisation already maintained such a force, but it was a message to EWE that the Anglican Church was ready to act unilaterally in the fight against occult threats.

A split may well have occurred in August if not for mediation by a Papal delegation and the Northern Sabbat.[15] By the end of that month, EWE was able to present to AREBaC protocols that restricted the entities that could contacted, restrictions on the terms that could be offered and protocols regulating summoning activities. An initial plan to restrict activities to contact rather than summoning was rejected, it being felt that the act of summoning was evidence to an entity that those responsible possessed some power over it. AREBaC were further placated by the fact that any summoning was to be an exercise in diplomacy rather than an attempt to directly involve the entities. The entities were to be selected from a list approved by a team

---

[15] The Northern Sabbat initially supported EWE's efforts but would later withdraw this support.

drawn from AREBaC, a Papal delegation and the ICG. The ICG'ss approval was deemed critical as it had suffered significant loses of personnel during Pantheon.

It is unclear as to whether the protocols alone would have been sufficient to sway AREBaC. Final approval was only secured following reports of similar consultations in Germany, involving the Thule Society, certain Bishops and Vichy Occultists. These reports were deliberately exaggerated by EWE and they achieved the desired effect. Johnson wrote cryptically to a Papal representative that

> the difference between a deal with the devil and a deal with a devil may be enough given the current strategic situation. May the Lord have mercy on us

On the night of 3 September 1940, mystics from EWE's E Office and the Armitage Institute gathered at a site in Southern England. In accordance with the protocols approved by AREBaC, the location of the site remains permanently classified, although. However, it was almost certainly a stone circle in southern England.[16] The first of the so so-called Operation Charon entities was duly summoned and given the identifier Charon Alpha. This first meeting was considered successful and was described by in the official EWE account as 'offering grounds for optimism and a building block for future relations'. The terms of an interim agreement promised support:

---

[16] The most probable location of the circle used in initial contacts was either Dartmoor or, most likely, Bodmin Moor in south west England.

in military matters surrounding the issue of defense against invasion. The terms of [REDACTED] having been deemed acceptable and can be dismissed as casualties inflicted by the enemy. [REDACTED] this may have further propaganda benefits given the ages although it is expected that the some may be happier to see those designated drawn from colonies.

Charon Alpha was again summoned on 14 October. This was reportedly to renegotiate terms, although most relevant documentation remains sealed. One of the few available documents was a report from James Wiseman, a warlock of the ICG, who noted

> have no doubt that they [AREBaC] are fully committed. They are complicit as are we all in meeting its demands. The difference is that while they weep of the souls given, we recognized recognised from the beginning that sacrifices in every sense would need to be made. I caution that we should not attempt to soften the blow to our own sensibilities through in any way reneging on agreements, no matter how slight

It may well have been that AREBaC (and likely some of EWE's leadership) were having second thoughts about Charon and the agreements they had entered into.

A little over one month later, on 15 November, Charon Alpha was again summoned. This summoning was somewhat hurried and protocols were not followed. In particular, not all of the required AREBaC and Vatican personnel were present. The reason for such haste is unclear, although in a letter dated two days afterwards Chaplain Johnson ominously wrote to the AREBaC legate in Bengal that

> we can't risk another Coventry. EWE has requested that [Charon Alpha's] tithe of persons be met from your region and have suggested Artemis be reactivated. Act accordingly.

The reference to Coventry was particularly ominous as the third, unscheduled summoning had occurred the day after the devastating German bombing of that city. Combine with Wiseman's warning concerning agreements made after the October event, it is possible to conjecture that the British, unhappy with the terms of the Charon Alpha agreement, had at least in part attempted to back out, the price being the destruction of Coventry.

Officially the Luftwaffe raid had succeeded due to effective guidance from the *X-Gerat* system. However, the aircraft of Kampfgruppe 100, who led the raid, included in their crews a number of mystics deployed as part of the Luftwaffe's Operation *Bronzepfeil*. *Bronzepfeil* was intended to enhance bombing through the use of hexes and manipulative spells. It was considered to be unsuccessful and discontinued in the summer of 1941. In almost every trial, the assigned mystics had found their efforts too easily nullified by counter measures or otherwise unable to significantly influence the outcome of raids. Conversely, on the night of 14 November 1940, it was noted in the *Bronzepfeil* diary that

British counters non-existent. All four personnel assigned to *Mondscheinsonate* [Moonlight Sonata — the bombing of Coventry] report clarity of vision of target from North Sea and unprecedented ability to influence attack through successful employment of offensive hexes. Post Post-raid remote viewing similarly unimpeded. Our most successful operation to date. All parameters are to be examined to facilitate repeat.

No similar success was ever again achieved using *Bronzepfeil* despite extensive analysis by both Walküre and the Ahnenerbe. Johnson's letter of 17 November suggested that the British were aware that reluctance to meet the terms agreed with Charon Alpha had resulted in its intervention. The extensive destruction wrought to Coventry's cathedral perhaps further underlined the nature of the forces being invoked by Operation Charon.

Alpha was not the only entity to be summoned or contacted through Charon. Precise details are difficult to ascertain as the relevant files remain highly classified. It has also emerged that a number of records may have been destroyed at the request of AREBaC in 1946 and the Vatican in 1985. A full analysis is also hindered by the fact that a number of minor or insubstantial contacts were made through Operation Charon. It has also been postulated that some of entities may have been different aspects of the same being. Thus, any list of contacts remains speculative.

Figure 6 gives an indication of the scope of Charon but does not include a number of unsuccessful summoning attempts. It also excludes summonings conducted by other agencies in relation to the main Charon efforts. Summonings of Charon Justicar and Charon Scepter were initially overseen by EWE as part of Operation Charon.

Codename	Number of times summoned Summonings (1939–45)	Location
Charon Alpha	4	Britain
Charon Cromwell	3	Britain
Charon Sulfuris	1	Libya
Charon Imperator	4	Britain
Charon Justicar	2	Britain
Charon Sceptre	1	Britain
Charon Bravo	2	Palestine/Iraq
Charon IV	1	Australia
Charon Orion	3	USA/Guyana
Charon T	1	Germany
Charon Guardian	2	China/India
Charon Regal	1	Netherlands
Charon Regent	2	Antarctica
Verified contacts with unidentified entities		4

Figure 6: Entities confirmed to have been contacted through Operation Charon, 1940 to 1945

From October 1941 responsibility for this passed to the joint EOG and OOE Project Trebuchet.[17]

Direct US involvement in Operation Charon commenced in January 1942. Mystics from the US Navy's Sovereign Occult Warfare group provided counter counter-scrying capabilities to screen contact with the entity known as Charon Orion in Guyanna. Initially overseen by a joint EWE-Emerald group, responsibility for further contact

---

[17] Chapter 5

passed to Sovereign in June 1942. Subsequent contacts with the Orion entity were made at the research facility located at Point Pleasant, West Virginia. These resulted in the acquisition of a number of artefacts of extra-terrestrial origin. Studied by a team led by Nikola Tesla, the components vanished from the secure laboratory two days after his death in 1943.

The most extensive US contributions to Charon occurred through DExNA. The organisation was closely involved in dealings with the entity codenamed Charon Guardian and orchestrated a meeting between Guardian and a team from the Los Alamos laboratory in January 1944. This occurred in India and included the gifting to the Los Alamos team elements of a Vimana weapon system.

A joint DExNA – EWE summoning was conducted in the Libyan desert during February 1943. The objective was to contact the entity codenamed Sulfuris. The entity had been identified in manuscripts recovered from Atlantis. It proved to be particularly hostile and the mission suffered twenty twenty-four casualties during a two two-hour battle in the ancient Djinn ruins of Halath. Loses included the EOG escort section and three observers from the ICG. The entity was eventually contained by a RMOWU team that was parachuted into the ruins. Sulfuris was held below ground within the ruins until a nearby Emerald coven arrived to carry out a banishment ritual.

One of the most enigmatic entities contacted through Charon was Charon Imperator. Unusually, Imperator had initiated contact. This had occurred when relations between the British and fae were at a particular low ebb. Indeed, it seemed as if EWE would face a war with the fae fae at the same time as one against Germany. Such was the level of fae apathy towards the British that the Thule Society persuaded Deputy Fuhrer Rudolf Hess, himself an occultist, to negotiate with them. On 10 May 1941, Hess landed in Scotland with a Thule advisor and a number of artefacts. His flight had avoided interception by the RAF due to interference from SS mystics operating in aircraft over the North Sea. At least so, it seemed. The reality was that EWE had also directed its mystics to prevent interception. Charon Imperator had notified EWE of contacts between the Thule Society and the fae. Hess entered the fae kingdom soon after arriving in Scotland but was ambushed by EWE operatives, and his Thule Society advisor killed.

While Hess was a prize himself, of more value to EWE were the artefacts that he had brought with him. This included Beowulf's shield, a map from aboriginal dream time and components recovered from a still unidentified spacecraft in Argentina. The fae response to the capture of Hess, a guest in their Kingdom, was outrage. Diplomacy and the gifting of the artefacts did little to abate this. It was only when the involvement of the Imperator entity became known to them that they became more compliant. E Office's chief diplomatic representative to the fae, noted:

> Although we owe Imperator a great deal, the precise
> capabilities of the entity remain unknown. The
> threat of its presence has been enough to intimidate
> the fae into complying with many of our demands.
> This has been enough to shift the stance of certain
> fae lords to friendly neutrality. Our personnel report
> heavy disruption to their abilities in Imperator's

proximity and a number of seers have been driven to suicide in its presence. The sense of foreboding it generates is remarkable, bordering on dread. I suggest a cautious approach in further dealings with the entity. In particular, until its motives are fully understood, we are to stress that the majority of faeare under our protection.

Initially Imperator had requested a fae kingdom over which to rule. The demand was refused on the grounds of recently negotiated treaties with the fae that guaranteed their security. Imperator's eventual price was to be no less than Hess himself.

E Office minutes concerning the final Imperator summoning in June 1942 record:

the former Deputy Fuhrer is to remain as an anchor to the material realm and for consumption following the destruction of his physical body after death. It is recommended that further negotiations with the entity do not proceed.

Hess remained a prisoner of the British, initially at the Tower of London before being moved to a secure location is Surrey. Following the Nuremburg trials Hess was moved to Spandau Prison in West Berlin. He was consumed by Imperator in 1971, after which he was replaced by a doppelganger until his 'death' in 1987.

The reasons for Imperator's interest in Hess, and the reason for the timing of the former Deputy Fuhrer's demise, remain unclear. A CBB investigation into Nazis occult activities found evidence of Hess' involvement in the summoning of 'a powerful and unidentified entity' in Prague during 1938. Reportedly, several of the gathered mystics were slain by the entity, descriptions of which match those of Imperator. If Hess was indeed present at this event, the reason for both his survival and eventual demise may be somehow linked.

Operation Charon achieved the goal of facilitating contact with powerful entities. The difficulty for EWE was that many of the entities could not be encouraged to act decisively. A number were apathetic towards humanity or, as demonstrated by Sulfuris, overtly hostile. Several were truly altruistic and sought to offer advice and guidance but, as ancient beings, were reluctant to become actively involved in mortal affairs. EWE were also wary that the motives of such beings could be unclear. In August 1943, Excalibur Operatives infiltrated the Silesian Coven of the Thule Society. They reported that both Charon Bravo and Guardian had been contacted by the SS. Charon T was not contacted through Charon until 1945, but it was known to have co-operated with the Ahnenerbe until contacted by the British in the Ruhr, and may have been contacted by the agents of the CBB in 1944.

Charon Regent was known to have been present in Japan in the days before and after the Japanese surrender. Post Post-war investigations by DExNA revealed that Regent was known to Imperial Japanese Army occultists as Golden Sentinel. They believed it to have been an entity worshipped by both the Zarlin and a related pre-human culture in Patagonia. During August and September 1945, a number of contacts took place between Regent/Golden

Sentinel and senior mystics from the IJA's Fūten organisation. Shortly after, the entity was reportedly summoned to a former Fūten facility in Manchuria, an event overseen by CBB operatives and members of the Soviet Navy's Vyriy group. The purposes of these contacts remain unknown, as does the extent of Soviet interest in the entities summoned through Operation Charon.

Chapter 5

Project Trebuchet

Through Operations Pantheon and Charon, Britain's occult warfare organisations had displayed a willingness to employ any means at their disposal. EWE had been the most enthusiastic in this, while the ICG and AREBaC had been wary in their involvement. The OOE and EOG had co-operated with Pantheon, and had a number of mystics and enchanters rendered unfit for service in doing so. In the aftermath both had refused to endorse Charon but agreed to provide security to 'prevent interference for public safety'. The OOE was also given observer status.

On 13 December 1940, a meeting was held between senior members of the OOE's summoning section, representatives of the RMOWU and a number of senior EOG personnel. Among the latter was Colonel Robert Mason, head of the EOG's Conventional Land Warfare Directorate. The directorate had only existed since June 1940, being tasked with researching how conventional weapons could be used to counter occult forces. With some justification, critics had argued that CLWD was a product of desperation caused by a shortage of occult resources available to the EOG. The purpose of the meeting was to discuss unease at the direction being taken by EWE and to discuss proposals of how to respond. There was a fear of furthering divisions in the British occult community (which had come to a head that September) and alienating the organisations of foreign countries operating in exile.[18] The minutes record that the meeting lasted nine hours. By the end, it was agreed that the OOE and EOG (through CLWD) would undertake joint research.

Mason was appointed to lead the project, to be codenamed Trebuchet. Its purpose was defined in instructions issued to Mason on 21 December 1940 as being to

> develop certain contingencies least an entity summoned through Operation Charon, or process of similar intent, should break its binding and resist banishment through mystical means. It is not to be considered as intended for general deployment amongst regular forces.

In many ways Mason was an ideal leader of such a project. He had studied the occult under North American tribes and had also served for six months with a units of EOG seers in Bengal. Mason had long advocated for an increased focus on non-mystical tactics to counter occult forces. Addressing a sabbat in Norfolk during February 1940, he had declared.

> I don't give damn if these things [occult beings] are dispelled or blown apart by a 4.5 inch shell. It will be one less for us to deal with.

However, while Mason understood the army and the occult, he had little scientific background. Thus a scientific advisor was appointed by the OOE, Dr Rachel Whitehead.

---

[18] See Chapter 7 'APIB's War'.

Whitehead was an occultist who had also developed in interest in psychology and biology. The daughter of a practitioner of Black Magic, Whitehead had conducted academic research in Northern England while also liaising with the Northern Sabbat. After studying in Spain, she had been recruited upon her return in 1940 by the OOE and tasked with managing one of its archives. Whitehead was considered a natural addition to the project due to her having managed the transfer of files relating to MI5's Guinevere group and Operation Castiel.

In 1926, Guinevere had commissioned research into the effectiveness of contemporary weapons against entities. Codenamed Castiel, its purpose was to enhance the capability of non-mystic field operatives to counter occult entities and beings. Conducted independently of EWE, the project had early on drawn criticism in British occult circles for a number of reasons. The decision to employ the American Michael Padalecki alienated many potential supporters. Padalecki studied under Tesla and in 1919 had joined the US Army's mystic unit 'Prairie Wendigo'. It is alleged that Padalecki had summoned and bound a thunderbird. This was then subject to experimentation as part of the controversial Winchester Study. The study took place at locations in West Virginia, Nevada and Florida.

The Winchester Study is suspected to have involved experimentation on a number of beings, including fae who are believed to have been sympathetic to mortals. Experiments reportedly involved a number of devices designed by Tesla specifically for the project, as well artefacts of Atlantean and extra-terrestrial origin. Many of the experiments were described as little more than torture, recorded as 'efforts to assess the vulnerability of certain beings and entities to physical forces'. The study was widely condemned in occult circles.[19] In 1930, the Vatican confirmed that it had 'destroyed or contained' all materials relating to the project 'on behalf of all concerned parties'. Nonetheless, elements of the research are believed to be held by British and French occult agencies.

There was growing realization realisation amongst occultists that Winchester and now Castiel threatened the preeminence of mystics in occult warfare. Thus Guinevere struggled to recruit mystics to its operation. Despite this, it was able to summon and bind a number of moderately powerful beings to support its research. Possibly the most significant was the giant Celtic boar Trwyd, which was summoned from its three thousand thousand-year slumber and contained with a coal mine. Here, it was subjected to a number of weapon tests involving different calibers calibres and ammunition types. There was indignation from both AREBaC and EWE when reports surfaced of Guinevere's activities. The senior Papal liaison to AREBaC, Geronimo Talgo, passed on the Vatican's 'gravest concerns'. Not only had the trials failed to produce significant results, but they also risked provoking backlash from fae kingdoms across Europe.

Organisations such as Guinevere were independent of EWE. But AREBaC and EWE were the cogs around which the occult apparatus of Britain turned. Both used their influence to bring put pressure on the leadership of

---

[19] After being ostracised by the occult community, a number of the research team found employment in either the Japanese Army's Unit 731 or France's UAMS programme.

Guinevere and the project was terminated in 1931. Padalecki returned to the United States to be recruited by DExNA. Guinevere was purged of its more radical elements and Trywd released. Details surrounding this are scant. The being had a reputation for rage and it is unlikely that it would have overlooked the abuses it had suffered. It is thus likely an arrangement was made between EWE and Trywd. A number of Guinevere personnel and their families disappear from the record at this time.

While EWE and AREBaC had closed down Castiel it was to be an EOG team that tracked down the files. EOG had remained silent in the widespread condemnation of the operation. It may have been that its leadership sought to capitalize capitalise on its findings. There were potential implications for military operations from any knowledge gained about the effect of firearms on faes. There is also evidence to suggest that EWE, while critical of the intent of Castiel, recognized recognised its value. A memo of June 1931 written by EWE's central committee to the head of H Office stated

> While it was desirable for the closure of a project as reckless as Castiel, it was ambitious in its scope and could potentially be of value. It is currently necessary to placate the church factions [AREBaC and the Vatican] but we must recognize recognise that any advantage that could be gained from Castiel should not be squandered. It is recommended that sympathetic parties be found who may later discretely assess the knowledge gained.

EWE had both the desire and opportunity to ensure the EOG received the data from Castiel. Whatever the case, the relevant files were acquired by the EOG's archive's department, and, through Whitehead, passed on to the Trebuchet team.

The Castiel files proved to be of some value. So to was the limited amount of information that Whitehead was able to track down concerning the Winchester Study. The result was that Mason and his team could determine small arms ammunition of sufficient caliber calibre could cause distress to certain fae beings (a fact already known and utilised by the RMOWU in particular). Some parts of them were more vulnerable to physical trauma than others. The Winchester Study also revealed that certain entities could, in theory, at least, be disrupted through electricity or magnetic fields. The significant breakthrough was, however, to occur in September 1941.

Whitehead had proved relentless in her efforts to track down documentation relating to both the Winchester Study and Castiel. Between February and August 1941, Whitehead travelled to the United States, Canada and Free French colonies in Africa. Her goal in the latter had been files transferred as part of Operation Blood Raven. By September, it was apparent that not only had the Castiel and Winchester researchers summoned entities to aid them, but they had, in fact, summoned the same entities. They had been identified as Granite and Cobalt by Guinevere when first summoned in 1928. To the consternation of the Trebuchet, both had been identified as entities of interest to Operation Charon.

It was no coincidence the Granite and Cobalt had been subject to the attentions of EWE. Renamed Charon Scepter and Charon Justicar, respectively, the entities were amongst the weakest summoned through Charon. That they were the same entities summoned to support Castiel had been recognized recognised by EWE. The decision had thus been taken to summon both to explore the potential of restarting the project. By 1941, the obstacle was not opposition from occultists but fear of a backlash from the face and, more importantly, a lack of resources. EWE gambled that granting access to the entities by the EOG and OOE would solve the latter problem, while the fae gave both organisations scant attention. At worst, EWE could bring pressure to bear as in 1931 and scupper the project in the name of fae and mortal relations.

Mason was too willy to believe that EWE offered Sceptre and Justicar purely to aid the war effort. Co-operation between the occult organisations of Britain was exemplary, but at this stage, Charon was very much a EWE operation. It was also clear that Trebuchet was an insurance should Charon fail. Despite this, Mason had little choice but to accept the opportunity. On 3 November 1941, Whitehead was again dispatched to the United States. This time, her mission was a not to retrieve information but to recruit the architect of the Winchester Study, Padalecki. By this stage, Padelecki had been promoted to the senior leadership of DExNA and was heavily involved in the bothboth the US Navy's experiments with invisibility and the Ocean Monarch leviathan programme.[20] Whitehead

---

[20] See Chapter 8 'Marine Leviathans'

returned without Padelecki in February 1942, by which time Trebuchet had moved into a new phase.

In the preceding December, Charon Scepter, now codenamed Leprus, was summoned to an army base on Salisbury Plain. To prevent the fae from discovering the project, the summoning was subject to intensive warding operations and other measures. Security was enhanced by teams from Vortigern, Styx and the RMOWU. Mason hoped that the entity would support his own efforts and he was not disappointed. Scepter claimed to have dominion over a number of lesser entities and beings that it could provide 'in return for co-operation if required at a later date'. Information concerning the purpose, nature and trigger of this co-operation remains classified. It has been speculated that Leprus may have been an entity with ambitions that could one day require the support of mortals. Equally, it may have been an entity with a penchant for mischief. In either case, it had little regard for its own kind and has evidently yet to ask for its reward.

Through a grimoire gifted by Leprus, mystics from Trebuchet summoned and bound a number of beings. Studies revealed them to be from a number of lesser fae races that were easily held and commanded by binding rituals. All were reluctant participants in what followed. A report written in April 1944 stated:

The beings have proved ideal test subjects and are easily commanded through the correct enchantment. Containment is simple through the correct application of any number of sigils and wards. They are in great number and this has enabled us to fully assess the lethality of various weapons and methods. Disposal of them has largely been achieved through banishment to the home realm at time of death, although those beings of a more mortal nature have required more conventional methods of disposal. I point to our efforts to do so in the Irish Sea. We have also achieved some success by using them as a food source in the training of barghests and werebeasts for security duties.[21]

Security was intensive and designed to deter both enemy and fae interference. There was a significant fear of the latter gaining knowledge of the test subjects and the diplomatic fallout that would inevitably follow. A coven drawn from RMOWU and OOE personnel was created to oversee operations against scrying and other forms of remote observation. This was to be the first large large-scale deployment of EOG's psychic warfare detachment. Plans were drawn up to request element's of APIB's C Flight for aerial security, but Mason intervened directly to postpone the plan. It was feared that the involvement of too many organisations would undermine both the security and control of the project.

To maintain secrecy, it was intended to construct the testing facility to resemble a reserve airstrip. The pens that housed the beings were designed to resemble hangars. Wardings and runes were embedded within the structures to support the binding of the beings and deter enemy remote

---

[21] The use of barghests and werebeasts was discontinued at the installation in December 1944, following an unfortunate incident involving ship wrecked fishermen.

sensing. This element was directed by Norwegian and Finnish rune smiths from the OOE. An advantage of using the cover of a reserve airstrip was that a variety of flights and aircraft types could land to bring in supplies. In the initial phase, this predominantly consisted of especially procured Avro Anson's and Wellington bombers in Coastal Command markings. An old jetty on the north tip of the island had been used to allow flying boats and vessels to unload. In January 1942, a new jetty was constructed next to the airstrip.

A variety of weapons were transported to the island for testing. This included small arms and the latest models of anti-tank weapons, notably PIAT projectors, bazookas and 6 6-pounder anti-tank guns. In 1944 a Valentine tank and Daimler scout car would be added to test firing 'in mobile conditions'. This proved unfeasible due to the difficult terrain on the island. Due to the limited resources available it had been intended that Trebuchet would operate in separate phases. This was scaled up into a more ambitious scheme of simultaneous testing programmes starting in June 1942. The catalyst was additional manpower becoming available due to the activation of the EOG's French-Canadian section.

Trebuchet Blue and Green both produced inconclusive results. As Operation Castiel had demonstrated, damage could be inflicted by conventional weapons. This was at the point where the magical energies that bound the creature's for was were weakest. Analysis of this data led to what was perhaps Trebuchet's most significant contributions to the understanding of beings such as the fae.

Codename	Weapons tested
Trebuchet Blue	Anti-tank and calibres above 1.5 inches (40mm)
Trebuchet Green	Small arms
Trebuchet Orange	Biological weapons
Trebuchet Red	Chemical weapons
Trebuchet Violet	High calibre weapons and blast effects
Trebuchet Gold	Counter entity attacks
Trebuchet Yellow	Atomic bomb research
Trebuchet Indigo	Extra-terrestrial and pre-human technology

Figure 7: Sub-programmes of Project Trebuchet, 1942 to 1945

One of the great enigmas concerning occult beings had been how they exhibited varying levels of resistance to weapons such as blades and firearms. Significantly there existed not only variations in the vulnerability of races, but also between individuals of the same race. Until the early twentieth century, it remained an almost unresearched phenomenon.

There are indications that certain pre-Incan cultures of South America, along with early Sumeria, had some understanding of this. The scant evidence that remains suggests that this had been passed on through extra-terrestrial sources. The first attempt of modern times to study the phenomena was conducted by the Knights Templar during the sixteenth century. This ultimately achieved little as within three months, those responsible were excommunicated for heresy, and a number of them burnt at the stake. Religious dogma hindered a later effort by the Vatican's secretive Order of St Eustace. Conducted in the period 1725 to 1736, this study benefitted from the scientific approaches of the Age of Enlightenment. However, due to the conservatism of the Catholic Church, the study had been unable to attract open scientific minds of sufficient caliber calibre to achieve results. In consequence the work focused on traditional occult methods and enchanted weapons.

During the nineteenth and early twentieth centuries, there was general acceptance and knowledge of advances in scientific methods and technology.[22] This enabled increasing co-operation between occultists and scientists. By the middle of the twentieth century, science had advanced to a point at which it could measure and monitor magical energy. It was this that made possible a major breakthrough by Trebuchet's scientists: a magical energy, acting something like a shield, gave the fae and others varying degrees of invulnerability to physical attacks.

In August 1943, it was discovered that this energy had a 60% commonality with the energy that composed many entities. For Trebuchet's main goal, of assessing the vulnerability of magical beings and creatures to gunfire, the essential finding was that this energy flowed inconsistently around such beings. Effectively, the weak points could vary from moment to moment. The core of these beings, however, retained a degree of resistance to attack. The precise level of resistance depended on the specific type of being. This explained an aspect of fae that had long baffled scientists and had been identified during Castiel: there was sometimes little difference in the damage inflicted by higher

---

[22] Although the unwillingness of the scientific community also held back research. A promising study commissioned by mystics in the Royal Navy was cut short in 1834 following the ridicule and subsequent suicide of the scientist involved.

and lower calibre projectiles on such beings. In effect, if a projectile got through the outer layer of protective energies, it would inflict damage but the damage was limited by the latent energies from which the target was constituted. Thus, with some beings, an anti-tank shell could thus thus do as much damage as a low low-calibercalibre bullet. A contradiction of the laws of physics, it was a constraint that Trebuchet needed to circumvent.

Mason's response was perhaps inevitable but an example of why he was the perfect leader for Trebuchet. In October 1943, he issued a directive to Trebuchet Blue and Green:

> It is now apparent that in regard to projectiles the what is far less a factor than how much. One hundred 303 rounds have more chance of finding a weak point than a single armor armour-piercing shell. A hit of any calibre in the right place may have as much effect as a larger munition. Hit them with everything.

It was, in many ways an implementation of the tactic long applied to werecreatures and vampires. Such creatures, however, had proved far more vulnerable than the fae. The logic behind Mason's directive was also that which had caused occult beings to suffer during the First World War: the volume of fire on the twentieth twentieth-century battlefield made it inevitable that something would get through.

Following the implementation of the directive, there was some increase in the damage inflicted on the test subjects. The findings were shared with Excalibur, the RMOWU and OOE. By emphasizing emphasising the volume of fire through automatic weapons, it became possible to achieve a limited but useful increase in the ability of occult beings to be countered by firearms. The result was that by April 1945, the standard organisation for EOG and Excalibur field sections was a four four-man team equipped with Sten or Thompson sub machine guns. The unit was trained so that each fired at a different part of the target to maximise the chance of hitting an unscreened area. It was a tactic that proved effective and has continued into the twenty twenty-first century.

Trebuchet Violet was an attempt to analyze analyse the effects of explosions on occult beings. Of particular interest was the effect of blast waves. In February 1944, a Royal Navy destroyer and cruiser unwittingly took part in these tests by conducting live firing against a supposedly empty island. It was found that blasts of sufficient force could disorientate the targets or disrupt the energies that shielded them. Trebuchet Gold was an extension of Trebuchet Violet that tested the effects of explosions on non-corporeal entities.

By their nature, entities were immune to physical attack. It was found that a sufficient number of explosions, releasing enough force at the correct moment, could potentially prevent a summoned entity from forming. Trebuchet Gold had been conducted against lesser entities. In 1945, plans were made to conduct tests against a more powerful entity, formerly known as Charon Justicar, in South Africa. Proposals were dropped as the risk of reprisal was considered too high. Ultimately, both Trebuchet Violet and Gold showed promised but required a high volume of explosives to arrive on target. In the case of Gold, this fire needed to be delivered almost simultaneously. The conclusions were summed up by the senior RMOWU liaison to Trebuchet in January 1945: 'It will be simpler for the damn things to manifest and then be dispelled rather than level a whole street'.

From late 1942, groups of the test subjects were subjected to trials involving chemical and biological agents. The former were was noted has having a very limited effect unless the target was significantly weakened prior to exposure. Of the agents tested, brucellosis was found to be the most effective. Chemical agents included phosgene, chlorine, mustard and cyanide. It was found that a combination of mustard gas followed by a cyanide-based blood agent could be effective against lesser entities. Details of the combination, designated Burnt Yew, remain classified. Plan Red-Violet combined a high explosive bombardment with chemical shells of different types. Biological weapons were found to be entirely ineffective.[23]

Trebuchet Yellow was an attempt to estimate the effects of a nuclear explosion on occult beings. This remained theoretical due to the slow production of atomic bombs that prevented testing. In an effort to gather data, an attempt was made by a joint DExNA-EOG mission to summon an entity to Nagasaki for the second atomic bombing. This was thwarted by Japanese mystics. Active testing commenced in 1953 in conjunction with Britain's nuclear programme.

---

[23] This was contradicted by research conducted by Japanese Army's Fūten unit. It has been reported that a hybrid pathogen was developed for the purpose. It is likely that this was achieved with the co-operation of scientists formerly employed in the Winchester study. It is speculated that the formula was seized by a US team in 1945.

Trebuchet scientists were also involved in the US Castle Bravo test and, latterly, the atmospheric Starfish nuclear test in 1962.

Arcano-archaeologists had long recognised the role of advanced technologies in wars the fought between ancient cultures and occult enemies. Much of this was of extra-terrestrial origin but cultures such as Atlantis and the Zarlin had achieved significant technological breakthroughs. Trebuchet Indigo was intended to explore the applications of such technology. It was an ambitious proposal, not least because much of the technology was not understood or relied on partially complete or damaged artefacts. Many of these artefacts were of religious significance, their abilities being mistaken for divine powers or interventions. In consequence, many had been identified, but their whereabouts were unknown. Further to this, once located there would likely be efforts made by other organisations, friendly and enemy alike, to acquire them.

In January 1943, an OOE arcano-archaeological team in the Yucatan excavated a subterranean palace of an unknown, pre-human Sauroid culture. Among the artefacts recovered was a so so-called pyro-sphere, a brass sphere containing a bound fire elemental. The sphere proved impervious to efforts by the team's mystic to assess the strength of the elemental within. Three local witches began a ritual to see what was within it but fled shortly afterwards. The sphere was taken to the coast, where it was flown to Miami and then taken by rail to a DExNA facility in Georgia. An analyses analysis of glyphs suggested it was of extra-terrestrial origin, although the object continued to be impervious to mystic investigation. It was then transferred to Canada.

Here, First Nation Shaman were able to assess the elemental as being of considerable power but that it possessed 'an angry spirit'. They warned against proceeding and offered to contain it within an isolated burial mound.

A report on the sphere was made by the director of the OOE's regional office. The report made no mention of the Shaman's recommendations:

> The artefact provides an ideal opportunity for [Trebuchet] Violet testing. There has been slight difficulty determining the nature of the entity within. This is due to the artefact being of extra-terrestrial origin. Nonetheless it should be easily contained.

The sphere arrived in Liverpool from Halifax that February. It was by now apparent that Trebuchet had in its possession a potentially powerful artefact. By the end of the month, its mystics were finally able to penetrate the wardings around the sphere and identify the entity contained within. With this knowledge, it was proposed to rebind the elemental. Once released, it would be commanded to rapidly expend its energies, creating a ball of fire. The proposal was that the sphere would be air air-dropped and activated above the target, creating an airburst effect. It would prove to be a plan created from hubris, and one that would have tragic consequences.

It was soon determined that the aircraft types available to Trebuchet were unsuited to the task. What was needed was a single single-engine attack aircraft. To maintain operational security, it was decided to make use of aircraft operating in the area. Through contacts in the admiralty permission was given to utilise a Fairey Swordfish of 816 squadron, then embarked on the escort carrier HMS Dasher. The carrier was working up to operational readiness at the mouth of the River Clyde following damage caused by severe weather while escorting a convoy.

A Trebuchet team arrived aboard the Dasher on the morning of 27 March. Their liaison was an officer recruited through blackmail. The team included a three three-man aircrew posing as trainees from a different squadron, two armourers and a navigator (in fact, a mystic). All were RMOWU personnel. The sphere was to have been placed within the casing of an air air-dropped sea mine for carriage to the target. The drop was scheduled for later in the day. However, by late afternoon, it was decided to postpone the operation 'due to inexplicable distortions of the sphere's form and disturbing emanations from within that were of a mystic nature'. Shortly after 1640, an explosion ripped through the vessel and by 1648, it had sunk. Of Dasher's 528 crew, 379 were lost.

A black out on the incident was imposed by the Admiralty. The subsequent board of enquiry concluded that the explosion had likely been caused by a fuel leak. Rumors began to circulate in the locality of the incident. There were reports of bodies buried in mass graves, of a naval vessel being salvaged and that an aircraft had landed on the vessel shortly before the explosion. All were denied by the Royal Navy. It was a situation that suited both the OOE and the EOG. Both organisations were aware of the true course of events, the operation having been observed remotely. Moments before the 'distortions' and 'emanations' were reported, an EOG coven reported that 'a presence of considerable strength' had penetrated the protective wardings and enchantments. The presence had then physically manifested itself aboard the vessel. Soon after, at approximately 1635, the RMOWU team made the following report:

> Suspected Cuckoo [code word for possession] event involving naval rating. Engaged unsuccessfully. Artefact remains secure. Hostile appears to intend to retrieve artefact.

It was the last message received from the team, who perished in the sinking. It seemed apparent that an entity had manifested itself aboard the vessel despite intensive screening efforts. It then possessed one of the crew in an attempt to retrieve the artefact. It was a simple explanation. Too simple for the OOE team tasked to investigate the incident. Its leader, Julian Grainger, noted:

> It was apparent from the start that there was something wrong with the course of events. That two experienced armorers had proved unable to the sphere after a week of practice using a dummy casing defies explanation. Even more remarkable was the reports of distortions to the sphere. It was when we investigated the emanations that the picture became clear. The operation had been the victim of outside manipulation.

The emanations were identified as being nearly identical to those used to summon Charon Sulfuris the previous month. This was just one of several links to the entity with which a battle had been fought in Libya during the previous month.[24] Further to this, a witness report of a survivor from the vessel matched that of a reported possession by the entity in Libya. In both cases, the possession had brought about horrific physical as well as mental changes to the victim. The witness from Dasher's crew was terminated and the body was used in the Operation Mincemeat deception.

The final evidence linking the loss of the Dasher to the Sulfuris entity was the identity of the six RMOWU personnel aboard the vessel. They were the final survivors of the team that had fought Sulfuris. The remainder had been killed in various 'operational accidents' in the preceding weeks, as had most of the Emerald team involved in the Libya operation. The RMOWU unit were not the only casualties sustained by Trebuchet personnel during the operation. An Anson had been airborne in the vicinity with a coven to shield the operation from both remote sensing efforts by the Ahnenerbe, and the attentions of the fae. The activation of the sphere had released a mass of charged energy that had struck the aircraft. This had caused both engines to fail. Out of control, it had struck the carrier, giving rise to rumors that the explosion had been caused by an aircraft. Amongst those on board were the two survivors of the emerald team that had fought Sulfuris in the previous month.

Despite the cause of the engine failure being known, the crash of the Anson could have been considered an

---

[24] See Chapter 5 'Operation Charon'.

unlucky fluke. It should have crashed on nearby land or into the sea. For Grainger it was one of many too coincidences surrounding the loss of the Dasher. Grainger's report concluded:

> the casualties sustained by the RMOWU team, and the involvement of the entity were inevitably beyond mere coincidence. There was clearly an intelligence at work. That intelligence was the entity known as Sulfuris. There is every indication that the event was engineered early on, possibly as back far at the point of the sphere's discovery in the Americas. I draw attention to the fact that the sphere likely provided a beacon upon which the entity descended. It is my recommendation that the team responsible be retired as one or more are likely compromised, vulnerable to manipulation or are a still active gateway.

Two days later, the archaeological team was recalled from a site in Patagonia. The aircraft carrying them exploded en route with no survivors.

It was not the end of the Dasher affair. RMOWU divers arrived on the scene to survey the wreck in an effort to either recover the sphere or confirm its destruction. The effort was supported by a tribe of Mers who successfully used scrying techniques to recover shards of the shattered sphere. The Mers also helped to drag a section of the vessel ashore. It contained the remains of both the RMOWU personnel and, it was hoped, that of the possessed sailor. This gave rise to rumours of the vessel being salvaged. The recovery of the

RMOWU team was a success and a precaution to retain secrecy. The body of the sailor remained unidentified. Grainger now faced a dilemma. He considered it likely that the sailor would have been horrifically disfigured, his transformation such that if washed ashore, it could create panic. Conversely, continued investigation risked drawing attention to the operation and difficult questions. It was Whitehead who resolved the issue in orders issued to Grainger.

> The recovery of the individual bearing the marks of the Sulfuris entity is to be considered a priority. It is highly likely to provide useful test material for both Trebuchet Orange and Red, while samples are also required for Yellow.

The result was a continued effort to search the wreck and surrounding waters. Around 50 bodies were brought ashore for examination at the nearby town of Ardrossan. Examination identified the sailor, while others were found to show signs of physical abnormalities caused by contact with the entity. Two bodies were used to provide samples for Trebuchet, whilst the remainder were burnt before being buried in a mass grave.

The involvement of Sulfuris was to have a significant impact on Trebuchet's programme. Mason remarked coldly:

> it played us for fools. The extent of its infiltration and influence may never be known.

As a result, plans to expand testing to entities of similar power to those associated with Operation Charon were abandoned. This included the proposal to incorporate Charon Justicar in to the Trebuchet Gold programme.

The pyro-sphere was not the only object tested through Trebuchet Indigo. A total of twelve artefacts were used, eight of them components recovered from crashed spacecraft. These were gained through co-operation with APIB and included several direct energy weapons. Results showed promise, but it was apparent that without an adequate power source the weapons would not achieve their full potential. In March 1945, Trebuchet supported an APIB-led recovery of a crashed extra-terrestrial craft from the sea west of the Shetlands. The craft, of unknown origin, had been brought down by a long long-range interceptor of the Yarl race. Both crew were passed to the Yarl but Trebuchet scientists were able to test the small arms found aboard. These were based on a sonic technology that proved effective. The results of the trial were used as the basis of the covert 'Squawk Box' weapons programme.

Some effort was made to emulate the use of electricity conducted in the Winchester Study. This was initially facilitated through the use of two capacitors recovered from a Nephilim temple, located 200 miles south west of Mosul. The report on the tests concluded:

> Containment of entities was achieved and it seems likely that disruption of manifestation is achievable. Despite these findings, electrical attack should not be considered a reliable counter measure to most occult beings once they are fully established. It may,

however be the case that other means of executing this form of attack can achieve more substantial results.

The 'other means' referred to in the report were ancient and religious artefacts that Trebuchet believed utilised a form of electrical discharge. Personnel from Trebuchet were assigned to the teams working with Mjolnir to investigate this phenomenon. During September 1943 negotiations were opened with DExNA to gain access to the Ark of Covenant, then held within a secure facility beneath Nevada. A preliminary agreement was reached for the artefact to be transferred temporarily to a facility in central Canada. However, objections raised by the archaeologist who recovered the Ark prevented this.

In February 1944, OOE operatives retrieved a shard from the shaft of the Holy Lance, then held in an SS Black Sun facility in Western Poland. Standard operating practice required that a small sample from such an artefact would be studied. Despite this, authorisation was given for the shard to be incorporated into ammunition of .303 caliber. This was found to be effective but efforts to locate further samples proved unsuccessful. This was in no small part due to a growing awareness in German occult circles that the Allies were conducting research into applying conventional weapons to occult threats. The intensity of the counter scrying and remote viewing activities surrounding Trebuchet had drawn attention to the operation. These same measures had prevented the Ahnenerbe from infiltrating remotely. In November 1942 O.Abt.K attempted to infiltrate a unit of Mers into Trebuchet's operating area. This proved unsuccessful, the unit being intercepted and consumed by werecreatures patrolling the island. A plan to reconnoiter using pro-Axis fae was thrawted thwarted by EWE's H Office two months later.

The Ahnenerbe was aware of occult activity in the area, but its precise nature remained unclear. Major Ludwig Kummer was responsible for efforts to conduct remote viewing of Trebuchet. Kummer was arrogant, unpopular with his subordinates and possessed in in a belief in the inferiority of Allied occult capabilities. He was nevertheless well connected and had been posted to a remote coven to avoid service in Russia. In his appraisal of the situation, he wrote:

> The purpose of activities in the islands to the west of Scotland remains unclear. It is apparent that the enemy view them as vital to the war effort and have mounted intensive counter counter-viewing operations. It is likely that these are nothing more than efforts by EWE to develop counter lycan munitions or similar. Krake's [O.Abt.K] efforts at infiltration have in all likelihood been intercepted by conventional British forces. We will continue to monitor the situation but expect no significant gain from expending further resources.

Kummer's false assumptions were compounded by own going failures of co-operation within Germany's occult warfare apparatus. On 2 March 1943, an agent of France's Sapphire defected to a field team of the Luftwaffe's Walküre in the Pyrenees. The agent was returned to Germany for interrogation, which revealed details Trebuchet Green, Gold and Violet. The information was held within Walküre and not disseminated as, according to the officer responsible:

> The intelligence does not reveal a significant threat to ongoing or planned [Walküre] operations. The capabilities of lycans and other were creatures are known and the enemy already has a number of viable counter measures in place. This intelligence will no doubt be of greater significance in the event of expanded entity operations.

The intelligence would have been of value to the SS Geisttruppen and may have significantly impacted Kummer's report. It was not until the destruction of the Dasher on 27 March that the significance of Trebuchet's activities became apparent. The release of the elemental and arrival of the Sulfuris entity in close proximity could not be fully masked by attempts to counter remote viewing.

A Luftwaffe coven in Norway made the following report on the incident:

> An event involving two significant entities has been detected to the north west of the British Isles. It appears our ability to measure the energy release was dampened by British warding efforts. However, initial estimates suggest an entity of some power was involved. It remains as yet unidentified.

The result was increased German efforts to breakthrough the warding and other protections in place around Trebuchet.

Security was substantial, but by the end of 1944, a humbled Kummer reported that:

> The enemy likely has a programme to enhance conventional weapons capabilities through occult means. It remains unclear if this is to increase effectiveness against our own conventional or occult forces. It is believed that efforts to acquire artefacts by the OOE maybe linked to the programme.

It was a reasonably accurate appraisal of the situation that lead to an increased focus on OOE operations to acquire artefacts for Trebuchet.

Despite extensive German efforts, the research element of Trebuchet remained uncompromised. Despite this, the extra attention on the operation would have one significant consequence. In February 1944, a Trebuchet team travelled to Northern India in an attempt to acquire the Kaladanda. Known colloquially as 'the staff of death', it had been theorized theorised that this may have been an energy weapon of pre-human technology. If so, the Kaladanda would have been of significant value to Trebuchet Indigo. The location of the artefact had been discovered by an EWE archaeology team as being beneath a newly discovered religious site of the Khasas' tribe close to the Burmese border. On 5 March, a Trebuchet team consisting of four researchers and a four four-strong escort section, drawn from the EOG, and three OOE mystics, arrived in the region. Interference caused by Japanese army mystics operating on the Burmese border had enabled an SS Gruppe Heimdall to sense both the team's arrival and the object's presence.

The gruppe had arrived at Singapore via U-boat in December 1942. Officially, its purpose was to conduct joint operations with Japanese occult units. Its commanding officer, Captain Michael Aubrecht, also had secret instructions:

> to acquire and return to the Reich artefacts that would provide advantage in the ongoing struggle against the Bolsheviks and Western powers. Your activities must also be governed by the knowledge that at some point a war may be waged between the German Reich and the Empire of Japan using all occult means at our disposal. To this end, it is to be considered paramount that such artefacts that cannot be dispatched to the Reich do not fall into the hands of other powers.

It was apparent that Aubrecht's superiors anticipated an all-out occult war with the Japanese Empire in the future. To this end, Aubrecht was instructed to destroy any artefacts of importance that could not safely returned to Germany. It was an order that demonstrated little understanding of operational realities. Gruppe Heimdall would be expected to keep any artefacts discovered secret from their Japanese allies, within whose territory they operated. These artefacts would then be loaded onto U-boats for the perilous journey to Europe. Aubrecht was no fool. He recognised the risk of alienating the Japanese allies upon whom his survival depended. He was also aware that the scientists and academics in his command would not stand by and witness the wanton destruction of occult artefacts. He thus adopted a policy of recording locations but not retrieving artefacts unless they were of significance. The latter would be retrieved and held by his unit to be used either as a bargaining tool or for defense. It was the later purpose that drew Aubretch's attention to the discovery of the Kaladanda.

Organisation	Role (number of personnel supplied)
Black Sun (SS)	Escort section/security (6) Signals (2)
Ahnenerbe (SS)	Mystics (2) Arcano-archaeology (1) Divination (1) Runesmith (1)
Walküre (Luftaffe)	Remote sensing and ether-communication (2)
Btl.SJ (Wehrmacht)	Lycan (tracker)
SS.Kp.K (SS)	Lycan (security)
Thule Society	Extra-terrestrial affairs (1) Arcano-archaeology (1) Arcano-biology (1)
Indian National Army	Mystic and counter mystic operations (2)
Imperial Japanese Army Unit 547	Mystic and counter mystic operations (4)

Figure 8: SS Gruppe Heimdall, 17 February 1944

Unusually, the gruppe consisted of personnel drawn from a number of Germany's occult organisations, as well as attached forces. This included organisations linked to the SS, Wehrmacht and Luftwaffe. The number of organisations represented in the group was in itself unusual for a German occult operation. More so was the fact that the unit appears to have operated as a coherent whole, unhindered by the rivalries that plagued Germany's occult strategy. This was due to both Aubrecht's leadership and a unity brought about by a mistrust of their Japanese allies. The unit included a range of combat, occult and scientific capabilities. The designation of personnel also disguised the unit's combat potential. All of the Ahnenerbe, Walküre and IJA personnel were trained field operatives, in addition to their non-combat specialisms. Combat capability was further enhanced by the powerful enchantments available to them, along with a small collection of artefacts.

On 15 March 1944, the eleven strong Trebuchet team arrived at a valley ten miles south of the Kaladanda's location. Here, they were reinforced by eight Karen Tribesmen who had training alongside EOG units in Bengal. They included a werebeast and a mystic. All had hunted degenerate Yeti that dwelled in the caves of southern Burma. Shortly after midday, as they neared the site, the group was ambushed by a force from the Heimdall team. What followed would prove to be one of the bloodiest engagements between occult units of the war. The Black Sun and IJA contingents each included a light machine gun, in addition to rifles. The eleven members of the EOG and OOE present were each armed with submachine guns that were significantly out ranged. The tribesmen were better able to respond, but their rifles were antiquated. Within ten minutes, three of the EOG researchers and two of the escort section were dead and the one surviving OOE mystic badly wounded. These four survivors had been able to crawl to the cover of a bolder due to a shielding enchantment cast as the dyeing act of a mystic. Here, they were pinned down by enemy fire. The five surviving tribesmen, each wounded, had sought similar shelter.

The situation for the Trebuchet team appeared hopeless. Nevertheless, the need for a rapid infiltration had limited the ammunition that could be carried by the Heimdell force. Furthermore, Aubrecht had hoped the initial volleys would have effectively neutralised the British mystics, leaving his own to focus on concealing the ambush. It was a gamble that had failed but it was clear that his force occupied a superior position. Both German lycans were instructed to transmute as the Heimdall mystics sought to shroud their approach. Suspecting something of this nature, the Burmese mystic commanded their own werebeast into action. It would be referred to as a 'weretiger' in after-action reports, although the description is not entirely accurate. The OOE mystic had sensed the German shrouding effort and weakened it enough for the Burmese werebeast to sense the lycans. It emerged from behind the boulders, causing its foes to pause. What followed was recorded by one of the Ahnenerbe operatives present.

> I had served alongside our lycans in both Spain and France but had never seen a creature such as this. It was almost two and a half metres tall, tiger tiger-like in appearance. While the tattered remains of clothing hung from our lycans, the beast had simply exploded out of his. The wereform was an order of magnitude greater than the human. Our lycans were enraged, hungry for blood, their minds bent by the transformation and the serums we administered. What followed was folly. They leapt at the British creature, but it maintained the agility of a cat, dodging one which lay on the ground winded. The second lycan locked its teeth into its left shoulder. Oblivious to this, the enemy creature drew the fallen

lycan from the ground by its neck. By this time, firing had ceased so that we could watch the epic struggle. Even the vultures which had previously hovered to pick the fallen backed away. There was silence until it audibly snapped the lycan's neck. Sensing it was next, the final lycan tried to withdraw, only to be dismembered by the beast. We attempted to counter it with magic, but as it advanced towards us, several of my colleagues fled. The Japanese held firm but there was too little time to cast enchantments, while the enemy mystics had also been busy shielding the creature. The speed at which it moved defied its bulk, but eventually, automatic weapon fire brought it to its knees. It was a pause that gave the remaining enemy time to recovery. Our fleeing comrades were set upon by the tribesmen who fought with their usual savagery.

The engagement resulted in seven British deaths, along with five tribesmen, including one who died of their wounds. In total, four German and four Japanese of the twelve personnel committed were lost. Of the four survivors, two would be captured en route, and only two would return safely. Gruppe Heimdall was a spent force. The survivors would retire deeper into Burma then into Malaya, before surrendering to an EOG unit in 1945. After the engagement, the Trebuchet team recovered the Kaladanda. For reasons that remain unclear, the artefact remained at a secret facility in North West India until April 1945. At this point, it was loaded onto a cruiser for transport to Britain. The Kaladanda would never arrive at the intended destination. It was unloaded in Italian Somaliland before reaching the Suez

Canal and declared an object of interest for Operation Drawbridge.

Chapter 6

Contingencies: Portcullis and Drawbridge

By the end of 1943, Trebuchet had produced only limited results. Through the research, it had been possible to refine tactics that could used against occult beings. Nonetheless Trebuchet had been unable to provide a viable counter to the more powerful types of entities. This was a concern amongst senior figures in the occult community, who had become aware of Trebuchet's goals despite intensive security efforts. It was apparent to many of them that Britain's occult resources were becoming increasingly stretched and that occult operations would need to be curtailed without a swift victory. Between 17 and 19 January 1944, a meeting between the leaders of AREBaC, the ICG and Northern Sabbat was held at a country house in East Anglia. Also in attendance were representatives of the Vatican, the AUO, Sapphire, Emerald, APIB and a number of fae kingdoms.

It was determined that the greatest danger from a collapse of British occult capabilities was not increased enemy activity. Rather it was the threat posed by entities becoming unbound or new ones entering the areas of the mortal realm that were undefended. This was because of an increasing number of entities beings present in the United Kingdom, a situation arising from Operations Charon and Trebuchet. It was the view of the fae that the continual summoning of powerful entities, as well as the distorting effects of their presence, risked collapsing the barriers between realms. The growing points of weakness were being held together by the efforts of mystics who sensed the presence of such areas, while being unaware of the cause. As the threat grew, so too would the need for coordinating these efforts. Yet, should there be a collapse in occult capabilities, the required mystics may not be available and those that were maybe engaged in containing unbound entities.

The outcome of the gathering was the creation of two contingency plans that could be implemented should the threat of unbound entities increase. The first was codenamed Boatman. This required the withdrawal to the British Isles of all but the minimum number of mystics required to sustain operations against the Axis. These would reinforce the boundaries around the mortal realm and counter any rogue entities. The second plan was Portcullis. It was envisaged that this could happen independently of the first, possibly before the collapse occurred. Through Portcullis, key sites of magical energy in the British Isles would be depowered. This would deprive entities of sustenance but also hinder the abilities of remaining occult forces. It also relied significantly on the co-operation of the fae, about which a number of occultists were skeptical. Edward Kohler, the senior ICG warlock present, informed his superiors that:

> While I remain broadly supportive of the proposals, I must question the logic. Boatman is extremely high risk. It may denude our forces of support and hand the enemy the strategic initiative. Portcullis is of more value but too narrow in its scope. We need to recognize recognise that our realm is surrounded by many and I fear the scope is too limited. I urge a more robust and wider wide-ranging strategy, particularly if reports from Poland are confirmed.

The reference to Poland related to emerging evidence of Black Sun experiments with interdimensional technology. Evidently, Kohler's concerns were acknowledged as on 3 February, the gathering urgently reconvened. On this occasion, representatives from EWE, DExNA and Jade were also in attendance. The purpose was to discuss the status of Black Sun's project and its creation of the device known as *Die Glocke* (the Bell).

The existence of *Die Glocke* had first came to the attention of the AUO in September 1943. Its mystics reported intensive counter-scrying and remote remote-sensing activities at a site in the Polish region of Silesia. This included previously unseen runes and counter-psychic techniques believed to have been enhanced by extra-terrestrial technology. Efforts to insert operatives through astral projection resulted in the loss of six personnel. In December, a joint AUO-DExNA coven was destroyed when spirits from the unit SS.Kp.K located them using a still active astral link. The addition of Vortigern and Nedu team's from EWE prevented further large large-scale losses, but casualties continued to be sustained. On 21 May 1944 an APIB Mosquito was intercepted whilst conducting an airborne scrying operation close to the facility. This was the first operational mission by an Me262Z, a variant of the fighter utilising a bound entity as a rudimentary onboard computer. Such entities enhanced effectiveness only if they were co-operative and the type experienced a high accident rate.

It was apparent that the German's continued to expend considerable resources to maintain the secrecy of the operation. The first significant breakthrough for the Allies occurred on 12 November 1944 when a coven from ICG launched a powerful remote sensing effort by expending a number of Atlantean enchantment scrolls. The link was terminated abruptly when a number of hostile spirits were sensed trying to track down the coven. Nonetheless there had been sufficient time to see the object and gather sufficient information about its intended purpose. Further efforts followed, each enabling Allied occultists to gain a fuller understanding. This was transformed on 22 January 1944 when a member of the Vatican's Order of St Eustace infiltrated the site at which *Die Glocke* was based.

The Vatican had for centuries monitored the activities of occultists and occult groups across the globe. It had an established, informal network of agents that was covertly supported by the Catholic Church. There were also those formerly within its structure, including a unit of the Swiss Guard, exorcists, investigators and various orders. Through these networks, the Vatican had been able to infiltrate the occult organisations of both the Axis and the Allies. This was despite its officials being granted observer or advisor status within many Allied projects. The motivations for this remain unclear and there is little evidence of overt interference by the Vatican in such matters. The role appears to have been one of observation and the gathering of artefacts. The extent to which the activities of the Vatican in occult affairs was were recognised is unclear. A letter from EWEs's to AREBaC's home affairs committee stated:

It is desirable that the Vatican would at least act rather than issue mere condemnation or sometimes empty guidance. If rumours about the infiltration of enemy occult capability are true, then it is difficult to what impact, if any, a rises. That the Holy See should take such an interest in occult affairs yet remain so detached is an enigma. There is nothing but here say and rumour of real action. The exception, of course, is when a relic or object of interest comes to light. Then we see activity but it is that of a compulsion to acquire for seemingly no purpose other than the acquisition. I refer, of course the recent operation in the Sudan.

The reference to an operation in Sudan related to Operation Linesman in May 1943. Excalibur agents had located evidence of a race of human–avian hybrids that had lived on the banks of the Red Sea in pre-human times. This included artefacts such as stone tablets, weapons and two mummified remains. These artefacts were to be transported into Somaliland in a three three-vehicle convoy. The convoy was ambushed by a force of tribesmen and Europeans en route. The attackers escaped with the artefacts and three were later identified as members of the Swiss Guard's occult investigations unit. It was one of a number of operations conducted by the agents of the Vatican to retrieve 'artefacts of interest'.[25]

While R Office was dismissive of the Vatican's contribution to occult operations, there was concern at the highest levels of EWE at the Vatican's activities and their true purpose. There are unconfirmed rumours that EWE, APIB and the Northern Sabbat conducted a jointly co-ordinated purge amongst personnel following reports of Vatican infiltration. This was believed to have taken place as

---

[25] Such operations continue into the twenty first century. The CIA's occult operations team reported a number of similar incidents involving Vatican forces in Afghanistan prior to the US withdrawl in 2021.

part of a secret directive known as Damocles. Currently the only known reference exists in a cryptic passage from an EWE document concerning internal security. Written in October 1944, the following was recorded:

> Known and likely sources have now been rendered a non-concern. This has been achieved with higher collateral damage than expected and excess on the part of the sabbat. It is likely that the ritualistic nature of the terminations may result in unnecessary exposure without swift actions, despite the current availability of means and procedures. Disposal of internal personnel of interest to be achieved at current and future V-weapon target locations. It is suspected that another Damocles will not be required if the message is understood.

It has been speculated that the Vatican was not merely observing. Rather, it was gathering the information required to manipulate occult activity through subversion and coercion. It is also likely that methods such as psychic and magic magic-based manipulation were employed. It was non-uncommon for both Axis and Allied occultists to report interference from unrecognized unrecognised sources in their activities.

That the Vatican had infiltrated the occult programmes of the Axis became apparent when the findings of the Order of St. Eustace were presented to the occultists gathered on 3 February 1944. It appeared that *Die Glocke* had resulted from the development from of a chemical compound known as Xerum 525. The existence of such a chemical, believed to be a form of plasma, had been identified by DExNA analysts as being in development since 1942. It had initially been thought to be related to the Nazi's' nuclear weapons programme. However, sources within the Thule Society had revealed it to be a product created with the assistance of extra-terrestrials. Xerum 525 had been intended as a power source for various intercontinental rockets and stratospheric aircraft being developed for the SS by Black Sun. It had been combined with pre-human portal technology smuggled from Kurdistan via Turkey to create *Die Glocke*. The device itself was intended to break down the boundaries between the material and other realms. The Order of St Eustace reported:

> Experiments by Blacksun [sic.] have indicated the potential of the device to facilitate the mass summoning of entities. This is achieved by expanding gateways created through regular practices, although this is an as yet untested capability Based on our own experiments in this field using devices of similar design, it is believed to be capable of generating localised chrono-distortion. As yet, there is no evidence of awareness of this on the part of the Nazis, who instead view it as a power source with destructive potential. It is believed that the device itself is mobile and may have the ability to displace itself spatially. The range of this is capability is yet to be determined.[26]

---

[26] Chrono-distortion, a primitive form of time travel, was subject of only limited research such French experiments in the 1880s. US and Soviet programmes had 1919 and 1924 respectively, although the most advanced were those of the Vatican. These commenced in 1911 and utilised artefacts recovered from Peru the previous year.

It was apparent that *Die Glocke* was a device of considerable potential that was yet to become fully operational.

Anglo-French mystic Emma Taylor-Smith was one of two representatives from France's Jade organisation present. A specialist in the integration of extra-terrestrial technology into that earth, Taylor-Smith was tasked to lead a joint Jade-APIB-DExNA team. It was instructed to act 'with utmost urgency' to determine a likely estimate for *Die Glocke* to reach operational status. One week later, on 9 February, Taylor-Smith advised:

> The complexities of the technological integration, and ongoing testing of capabilities, indicates the device to be a threat in the medium to long term. It is unlikely to achieve operational status until the autumn. However, the deteriorating military situation in Silesia may compel a full activation of the device before testing is complete and safeguards prepared. Intelligence indicating efforts to stabilise the device using psychic energies released through the use of expendable subjects. Trials conducted by Sapphire in Africa demonstrate this to be a powerful but inconsistent source that itself has inherent dangers. Further to the risk possessed by a premature activation of the device, consideration is to be given to efforts to prevent its acquisition by the Soviets. This is particularly imperative given the likely compatibility of the device with artefacts recovered by the CBB from western Mongolia.

It was determined that the most likely and significant threat was an activation of *Die Glocke* without necessary safeguards. Such an event had the potential to trigger an influx of unbound and, thus, uncontrolled entities.

The response to the threat of *Die Glocke* was the strengthening and broadening of the Portcullis Plan. Operation Portcullis, as the original plan was now known, consisted of a number of targets close to the location of *Die Glocke*. As in the case of the original plan, it was intended to remove nearby sources of magical energy that could sustain an entity. These were identified through liaising with Polish occultists who had fled the Nazis occupation of their home nation, many of whom were now employed in British and French occult organisations. The original plan had primarily relied on the fae to depower key locations. However, the region was the location for intensive military operations, with many of the native fae having already gone into hiding to escape German persecution or to evade that expected from the Soviets. Given their precarious situation, it was also unclear how far the fae of Silesia and surrounded surrounding regions would be willing to acquiesce in the depowering (albeit temporarily) of sites upon which they relied. It was apparent that other means would be needed to neutralise the sites. To facilitate this, the sites were categorised by the committee tasked with coordinating Portcullis.

The distinction between depowering and deactivation within the categories was that the former relied on the physical destruction of the site. In the case of a forest copse, this could be achieved through an air attack. Conversely, certain megalithic structures would require a more precise attack by ground ground-based units, particularly in the case of artefacts housed within structures.

Category	Mode of depower/deactivating
I	Sites to be depowering by mystics from within Allied territory
II	Sites to be depowering by mystics with proximity
III	Sites to be deactivated by attack from ground forces
IV	Sites to be deactivated by bombing
V	Site that cannot be depowered without local support by the fae.

Figure 9: Categorisation of sites identified as being of interest to Operation Portcullis

The destruction of sites had been resisted by the fae but was ultimately accepted as a matter of necessity by them. In total it was estimated that there were six sites split between categories III and IV. These were to be struck by assets drawn from the USAAF Thunder Eagle unit, APIB's C Flight, Sapphire UAMS, Excalibur teams and RMOWU sections. It was considered that with sufficient remote support, such as screening and protective enchantments, the attacks would stand a good chance of success if they arrived at the target. Nonetheless, the location of the targets in central Europe would ensure that the chances for a successful return upon completion would, at best, be slim.

Portcullis was considered a high high-risk operation that was not implemented. An even more radical proposal was made by the OOE. Codenamed Operation Drawbridge, this was to be an attack on entities that had materialized materialised due to the deactivation of *Die Glocke*. This would have involved a co-ordinated assault on the entities by mystics in Allied territory, including operatives of the

CBB, and the mass deployment of Burnt Yew chemical agents. The operation was to be supported by elementals, Sapphire UAMS and RMOWU teams. The latter would have been supported by Excalibur operatives and the employment of a number of artefacts. Drawbridge was accepted as an option of last resort. It was strongly supported by the fae, the Vatican and AREBaC. All three saw it as a chance to implement a mass cull of what they believed to be troublesome and dangerous beings.

By March, the Soviets had over ran Silesia, *Die Glocke* and new prototypes being moved to new locations. Both Portcullis and Drawbridge remained at readiness and DExNA was known to have explored the potential of deploying both an atomic device and Mjolnir in support. Both operations were stood down in September 1946, when the final operational *Die Glocke* was secured by Anglo-US forces.

Chapter 7

APIB's War

The Air Phenomena Investigation Branch had been formed by the Royal Flying Corps during World War I. Due to its nature, the RFC was science and technology technology-orientated. There was, however, an awareness amongst some of its personnel that there existed phenomena that defied scientific explanation. Reports of encounters with flying creatures and unidentified aircraft were routinely dismissed as misidentification of clouds, birds or other aircraft. Pilots who persisted in investigations could find themselves regarded as dangerously unreliable, grounded or posted elsewhere. It was the latter that would contribute to the creation of APIB.

In March 1915, Lieutenant James Marsden was flying a training sortie over southern England. Having become disorientated in low cloud he was attempting to find his aerodrome in the failing evening light. What followed was recorded in his report:

It was like a dirigible but circular, I would estimate a hundred yards across. It remained stationery stationary in the cloud and I may have collided with it had it not been for the illuminations around its outside edge. White but also green. I went to pass it again fearing it was a Boche but it went straight upwards at amazing speed and disappeared into the night sky.

While skepticism remained the official policy of the RNAS, the Royal Navy had traditionally been more receptive to the notion of the occult. EWE personnel worked secretly but closely with all branches of the Royal Navy. In January 1916 an M Office investigator by the name of Thomas Scott became interested in Marsden's report. Scott was frustrated by EWE's lack of interest in possible extra-terrestrial craft and saw an opportunity to gather further evidence through by establishing links with the RFC.

EWE's influence enabled Scott to get Marsden transferred back to the RFC. In April 1916 he was posted to France and reported back to Scott incidents of occult phenomena. Inevitably, there was much hearsay, third third-hand accounts and misidentification, but for Scott, this was the norm in such investigations. There emerged a picture of widespread occult phenomena, some of which could be attributed to enemy activity. Ironically, it was to be incidents that were not caused by the enemy that would directly lead to the creation of APIB.

There had been growing concern in the RFC leadership about security at their bases in Britain and elsewhere. Sightings of apparitions by sleepy sentries was were hardly new, but they appeared to be increasing. There were also reports of lycans near aerodromes in France and 'large winged humanoids' encountered by a party of construction workers in Egypt. The policy of suppressing and discrediting reports continued successfully, but there was a grudging recognition that they needed to be investigated. Ultimately, only a handful of the incidents were genuine occult phenomena and none were the result of enemy activity.[27]

That reports of apparitions in RFC (not to mention army and naval) installations largely proved unfounded was little comfort to EWE. There was growing evidence of efforts by the occultists of the Central Powers to explore potential applications of their expertise to the battlefield. In Germany, military occult activity was focused in on the navy and naval air service. The latter included Walküre, Germany's principle occult organisation. Neither the German army (until 1917) nor the Austrian military had anything similar, but occult capability was provided by independent groups of occultists operating in isolation. An influential coven existed in the Turkish army that was known to be courting the Great Djinn of the Sahel, while Bulgaria had began begun to form a cadre of were-creatures in 1916 for deployment against Russia. Of great concern to EWE was that the Germanenorden (German Order) occult society was beginning to organise expeditions in an effort to recover artefacts from sites in Mesopotamia, central Asia and West Africa.

Although uncoordinated, these were threats that EWE could not ignore. Co-operation with the Royal Navy was effective, while the British army had several small occult organisations operating within its ranks. These would form the Esoteric Operations Committee in 1917, which would subsequently become the Esoteric Operations Group in 1930. Bolstering the occult capabilities of the RFC was a priority and in August 1916, EWE formed its C Office,

---

[27] The incident in Egypt proved to be the most significant and subsequently investigated as part of Operation Drawbridge in the 1944.

responsible for air warfare. The difficulty faced by EWE was that aviation was in its infancy and its mystics effectively had no knowledge of aircraft. The only option was to form an organisation consisting of RFC personnel who had an interest in the occult. Codenamed Wyvern, this initially consisted of 5 occultists (including Marsden) and a shaman recruited from East Africa.

Wyvern was dissolved after only a month and reformed under Captain Geoffrey Stanlaw as APIB. Stanlaw was an archaeologist and longtime proponent of links between prehuman and off off-world cultures. He had travelled extensively in South West Asia during the early 1900s, seeking evidence for his theories. In 1911 Stanlaw was recruited by EWE to investigate the remains of a supposed ruined city of the Shambhala culture, said to be located on the Azeri shores of the Caspian Sea. Later transferred to E Office, Stanlaw remained in the employ of EWE until volunteering for the RFC in 1914. Like EWE, Stanlaw was concerned at the growing threat of enemy occultists and used his influence to oversee the creation of APIB. It would become one the most progressive of Britain's occult warfare organisations.

Stanlaw continued as APIB's leader until his death in 1937. By this time, it had become responsible for one of the most ambitious projects outside of EWE's control: Project Myrddin . The project had been born from the prevalent concept of the era that 'the bomber would always get through'. Events of the Spanish Civil War would seemingly prove this concept. Never one for consorting with entities or the fae, Stanlaw's proposal was to explore the use of dragons in aerial warfare.

From the instigation of Myrddin in 1935 APIB teams had been sent to the Far East and South America to find suitable creatures. Those of South America proved too powerful to be awoken, many in this region being not true dragons but rather entities composed of magical energy. The dragons encountered by the mystics of APIB's China Station too, proved resistant to summoning efforts. When one was finally drawn from its cave in Northern Burma during August 1938 the APIB team was incinerated. It was thus those semi-mortal creatures slumbering in the Welsh hills that were found to offer the most potential.

The focus shifted to Britain, but teams supporting Myrrdin continued to be deployed overseas for a variety of purposes.

Number of teams	Location	Role
3	Britain	Research and preparation for summoning
1	Iceland	Research
1	Norway	Preliminary contact
1	Peru	Summoning
2	Western China & N. Burma	Summoning and preliminary contact
1	Australia	Aboriginal liaison

Figure 10: Teams assigned to Myrddin, January 1939

By January 1939, Myrddin accounted for approximately 70% of APIB's mystic resources. Still recovering from the loss of personnel in Burma and overstretched, APIB thus sought support from other organisations. EWE and the ICG each provided a small number of mystics. Initially, the army's EOG proved more reluctant but relented following pressure from its own covens. In February, the effort was further bolstered by Druidic elements of the Northern Sabbat. The increase in mystical capability was welcome, but not only had Myrddin effectively ceased to be solely an APIB operation, but the organisation remained over extended in almost every field.

The situation facing APIB had not gone unnoticed within EWE. Some of the longer longer-serving personnel (who now served in EWE's leadership) viewed Stanlaw's formation of APIB twenty twenty-three years earlier as an act of betrayal. Stanlaw had, after all, been trained by EWE. APIB was also seen to have a growing influence in occult circles, particularly following Elton's involvement in the activities of the Armitage Institute.[28] Finally, APIB was perceived as moving away from conventional occultism, taking an increasing interest in extra-terrestrials, psychic abilities and recovering lost technologies. This made APIB an ideal partner for the more traditional EWE. However, for EWE and other leading occultists, it demonstrated APIB to be a rival with a radical agenda.

On a rain-swept hillside in March 1939 a group of druids and members of the ICG gathered at midnight under APIB direction. This was in an effort to awaken a dragon. Mystic security to prevent remote or spirit observation was provided to the Vortigern group. Despite the best efforts of the Myrddin team, the dragon could not be awoken. Two weeks later another attempt was made and proved marginally more successful: the creature was awoken but proved to be uncooperative. It was to be a pattern repeated on the three further occasions that the Myrddin team attempted contact.

---

28 See Chapter 1 'Spirit and Beast Warfare'

It rapidly became apparent the dragons were too ancient and aloof to wish to help humans. Furthermore, unlike the Charon entities, they were mortal (albeit slightly) and thus had much to lose by reckless involvement in affairs that did not concern them. An attempt to bind a red dragon ended in disaster and the loss of twelve personnel in September 1940. APIB was discredited, its new approach to occult warfare seen as a failure. The covert support amongst the ruling establishment that was vital for occult organisations evaporated for APIB. Many of its occultists left the organisation and were recruited into EWE's M Office. C Office eagerly absorbed many of APIB's technical personnel. The organisation had become a victim of an event almost unique in British occult circles: a power struggle. It was a struggle between traditional and new thinking that had been won by the former. This would have far reaching consequences but would never be repeated.

APIB retained numerous core personnel and this enabled it to be re-structured during the spring of 1941. It was now organised into three flights. The role of C Flight continued to be combat operations, although this now included ground as well as air following the disbanding of T Flight.[29] M Flight was concerned with mystical operations, S Flight with extra-terrestrials. Of the three S flight represented APIBs greatest capability, the relevant personnel having largely escaped the attentions of EWE (which viewed extra-terrestrials as a distraction from its main aims). By the middle of 1941, M Flight had been able to counter most German attempts to enhance bombing through mystical means. As a result, Bronzepfeil had been discontinued in

---

[29] C Flight's ground warfare role would be given to the Incursion's Counter Measures Unit of the RAF upon its formation in 1955.

December 1940. [30] It was superseded by the joint Walküre-Thule project codenamed Operation Vel. The purpose of Vel, like subsequent operations of this nature, was to enhance bombing. A directive of January 1941 stated that this was to be achieved through:

    a.   The deception of enemy conventional defences

    b.   Disruption of defensive occult forces

    c.   Physical enhancement of bombing through manipulation

    d.   of falling ordnance and manipulation of outcomes

Vel differed from usual Germany occult activity by utilising non-European mystics. Primarily, those for Vel were drawn from Italian East Africa and the ranks of Indian Nationalists. The change in the type of enchantments enabled Vel to achieve limited success, with a marginal increase in accuracy. It was the view of Walküre analysts that this would have been greater had it not been improvements in conventional British defenses. In any case, the point was moot. Within six months, British mystics, led by M Flight, had nullified the capabilities provided through Vel.

Even though the strategic bombing effort against Britain was reduced from 1941, efforts by the Germans to increase the effectiveness of bombing through mystical means continued. Of note was that even after the invasion of the Soviet Union in June 1941, efforts continued to be focused on efforts against Britain. This did not go unnoticed by either C Office or APIB. A memo from EWE's C Office to the air warfare department of Free France's Emerald organisation, stated in November 1941 that:

---

[30] See Chapter 7 'APIB's War'

> It seems inconceivable that the enemy should devote so much of its mystical effort to the bombing of Britain when there is more pressing need in the East. It is our belief that a new enemy capability will shortly be deployed in that theatre and become evident. It may be that such a capability has the potential to dramatically shift the balance of the air war.

Intensive efforts in the following months would reveal reasons for the continued focus on Britain.

The Luftwaffe strength available for bombing Britain had been reduced to support operations. Significantly, the British had also increased the capabilities of their conventional defenses. Thus, mystic methods to support continued operations against Britain were seen as vital. There was, however, an additional reason for the focus of German occult efforts to support the bombing of Britain. The fact was that many German occultists did not adhere to Nazis racial theories and viewed the British as the traditional enemy. It was also recognised that the bombing of Britain had the potential to disrupt its occult activities and damage sacred sites.

Walküre's Operation Bronzepfeil II commenced in support of the so-called Baedeker Blitz of 1942. Bronzepfeil II utilised artefacts of the pre-human cultures.[31] Obtained through exchanges of occult materials with Japan, the artefacts were intended to increase the effectiveness of mystics deployed aboard bombers as 'observers'. With surprise, this may have been effective. Nevertheless, against

---

[31] A number of tablets from the lost civilisation of Mu were utilised, alongside a Codex from Argatha.

Ahnenerbe's advice, the artefacts had been loaded onto a single Japanese submarine in Sumatra during in October 1940.

The concentration of so much mystical energy aboard a single Japanese submarine had inevitably drawn the attention of Allied seers. Security was further undermined by the collective energy interfering with Japanese efforts to counter scrying and remote viewing. Such was the disruption that when the submarine refuelled at Singapore, AUO was able to momentarily place an operative on the vessel via astral projection. This, combined with intelligence gained by DExNA, enabled M Flight to identify the purpose of the artefacts and prepare counter measures accordingly.

Operation Bronzepfeil III attempted to emulate Vel by using a group of mystics recruited by the Ahnenerbe in the Dutch East Indies. The capabilities of this group was were easily countered by existing British mystic defenses, and their use was not even registered by M Flight until post post-war analysis of the relevant records. The focus of Bronzepfeil III was shifted to the Eastern Front and resulted in a slight increase in the effectiveness of German bombing. This lasted only two months due to the establishment of the Red Airforce's own mystic counter measures unit. Codenamed Domovoy the unit was based at Tula. Five of its initial twenty twenty-four personnel were loaned by APIB. Vel II was activated in May 1944 to support V-1 and, latterly, V-2 operations. Utilizing Utilising *K'lmar* technology that enabled remote thought-controlled guidance, the project showed promise. Ultimately, Allied conventional counter measures against the V-weapon offensive effectively nullified the advantages it offered.

In the final analysis, Walküre's efforts to support bombing through mystical means must be considered ineffective. At best, only short short-term, marginal successes were achieved. Oberst Christoph Fischer had overseen Bronzepfeil II and III. He reported to a gathering of senior Nazi mystics in September 1944 that:

> Since the commencement of Bronzepfeil I efforts have been consistently and effectively thwarted by effective Allied counter measures. It is my estimation that the RAF's APIB had an effective and well well-screened covert programme established before the war to nullify our efforts to enhance bombing operations. This was supported by the USAAF's Kinati and Deflector programmes [these were actually DExNA operations conducted in conjunction with the USAAF's Thunder Eagle occult unit]. It seems inevitable that mystic and extra-terrestrial counter measures were combined. Almost inevitably, the global reach of the Western Alliance has played a decisive role as their organisations possess a depth of knowledge and resources that even our own Ahnenerbe and [Thule/Vril] societies can only aspire too.

Fischer was acknowledging something that many German mystics had feared to voice since the outbreak of the war. Specifically that it was not the strength of the magics available to the Allies that enabled them to gain the upper hand but rather the variety of disciplines available. Each had strengths that could be used to counter occult operations, minimising the weaknesses of other available disciplines. Fischer, however, had dramatically over estimated the extent of APIB's pre-war preparations to counter programmes such as Bronzepfeil and Vel.

In 1940, an APIB team was established under the leadership of Squadron Leader Nicholas Huxley. Its task was to assess the role of German operations aimed at the mystical enhancement of bombing. Huxley was an occultist and collector of artefacts from ancient Tartary, who had also served with the RAF in Mesopotamia. In 1927 he had been present at the opening of an Anunaki tomb in an expedition led by EWE's R Office. Huxley then worked with APIB's Middle East section in a failed attempt to activate an energy weapon recovered from within the tomb. A keen advocate of using occult means to support Britain's war effort, Huxley was the ideal candidate to head such a team.

The evidence gathered by Huxley included analysis of reports on Luftwaffe actions in the Blitzkrieg, the bombing of Rotterdam and a French study on the Condor Legion in Spain. In August 1940, Huxley presented his final report, which proved remarkably accurate in its conclusions:

The fate of the Advanced Striking Force in France and subsequent Bomber Command operations clearly show that the bomber will not always get through. We can also safely conclude that against a defense of even moderate efficiency enhancement of bombing through mystical means will be effectively nullified.

The efforts of the enemy will invariably focus on efforts to improve accuracy through telekinetically manipulating the fall of bombs, manipulating patterns of chance through hexes and protecting bombers from conventional counter measures such as flak and fighters. Despite the views of the EWE#s Air Warfare Advisory Committee [EAWAC] I advocate in the strongest terms recognition that extra-terrestrial technology exchanges may fall into the category. I refer to the report by Wing Commander Raymond's in relation to the Calvine basing proposal.[32]

In all cases of attempts at enhancement, the advantage lies firmly with the organized organised defender as they will be able to focus a greater concentration of counter mysticism. Conversely, that available to the attacker will lack focus: either mystically capable crew will be scattered over a number of aircraft or concentrated at a single point, limiting effectiveness. This also brings with it the possibility of losing all such crew if the aircraft is hit, while casualties on the dispersed crew will also be heavily disruptive. It is also my belief that shielding against conventional attack will offer, at best, only a slight advantage. This is due to the disparity between the relevant capabilities of fighter and bomber aircraft. Tactical operations are too dynamic for offensive support to be effective. In short, even with no mystical counter, the mystically supported attacker has little to gain. Complacency should be avoided. We should not neglect our defensive capabilities, as even a marginal advantage may bring significant results for the enemy if pursued for a prolonged period.

---

[32] Raymond was a keen advocate of co-operation with extra-terrestrials. Joining APIB in 1917 he was eventually promoted to Group Captain. He served into old age and would become involved in time travel experiments during the 1980s. In 1940 he had advocated for the creation of a facility to host extra-terrestrials at the isolated Calvine airfield in Scotland.

> I continue to advocate mystical intelligence gathering and other disruptive operations away from the battlefield, be it on land or air, but cannot recommend a significant frontline deployment in an offensive role due to these short comings.

In addition to nullifying a questionable German capability, counter counter-enhancement operations provided training for mystics for several organisations. In the years 1943 to 1945, 70% of the army's EOG and Royal Navy's RMOWU received training in this way, in addition to almost all of OOE's operatives recruited from 1941.

Recognition of the futility of enhancement ensured only minimal mystical support for Bomber Command's operations over Europe. Support often focused on single aircraft, often remotely and without the knowledge of the crew. This was particularly in regard to photo reconnaissance operations. These remained vital as remote sensing, scrying and similar means remained too inconsistent to give accurate information. Support was also available for larger operations. For its most sensitive specialist missions. C Flight maintained a small force of aircraft. Airborne coven operations involved the carriage of M Flight and other mystics (including non-coven groups) and, therefore, required large transport types. The most common missions of such aircraft and their passengers were counter counter-scrying, remote sensing, guidance or long long-range remote communication. Other roles could include the carriage of emissaries of fae races, long long-range escort of extra-terrestrial emissaries or even as locations for the summoning of, or contact with, certain entities.

The demands of the conventional war effort significantly impacted the number of aircraft available to C Flight.

Despite this, it was able to build a small force of high high-performance aircraft with customised airframes. The types and numbers available to C Flight are shown below. The following abbreviations are used: AC (Airborne Coven), EO (elemental support operations), OC (Operation Charon), SC (Operation Sky Cage), PR (photo-reconnaissance), MP (maritime patrol) and LRR (long-range reconnaissance). Initially, Talos was the codename given to operations to prepare countermeasures against airborne weres and other beasts. From 1942, the role of Talos was expanded to include trials of weapons and tactics for use against aircraft of non-earth origin. From January to November 1944, Talos also included counter extra-terrestrial incursion and surveillance missions. These missions were codenamed Sky Cage from 1944. Figures 11a and b show the principle aircraft types used by APIB.

Type	Year	No.	Notes, including location and role (UK unless noted)
Blenheim	39–40	1	Reconnaissance, AC
Defiant		1	Chase aircraft for Myrrdin
Wellesley		1	Egypt: Reconnaissance, AC
Spitfire	1941	1	Middle East (India from December) PR, Talos
Beaufighter		1	AC, Talos
Wellington		2	LRR, MP, AC
Spitfire	1942	1	Talos, OC
Hurricane		2	Murmansk and Palestine: Talos
Beaufighter		2	Burma and UK: Talos, AC
Mosquito		2	PR
Catalina		1	Ceylon: Reconnaissance, MP, AC
Spitfire	1943	2	UK (2 seater)/Egpyt: Talos, OC
Hurricane		1	Murmansk: Talos
Beaufighter		2	India: Talos, AC
Moqsuito		2	Egypt/Italy, Talos, AC, OC
Mosquito		2	PR
Cataline		1	Reconnaissance, AC
Spitfire	1944	1	Two seater Egypt: Talos, SC
Beaufighter		3	UK, Burma (2): Talos, AC, OC
Moqsuito		2	Italy, UK: Talos, AC, LRR, EO
Mosquito		1	Boosted engines, SC
P51		1	UK/France: Talos
P38		1	China: Talos, SC
Attack Spheres		?	Presumed UK, Europe and Canada: Experimental technology
Mosquito		2	UK and France: PR
Catalina		1	Ceylon: Reconnaissance, MP,AC

Figure 11a: APIB C Flight combat aircraft 1939 to 1944

Type	Year	No.	Notes, including location and role (UK unless noted)
Firefly		2	Burma, UK: AC, EO
Spitfire		1	Talos, SC
Mosquito		2	Belgium: Talos, SC, EO
Mosquito		3	UK (1), Yugoslavia (2): SC
P38		1	China: Talos, SC
Meteor	1945	1	Fitted with Yarl equipment: Talos, SC
Meteor		1	Belgium: reconnaissance
Attack Spheres		?	Presumed UK, Europe, Australia and Canada: Experimental technology
Mosquito		2	PR
Catalina		1	Ceylon: Reconnaissance, MP, AC

Figure 11b: APIB C Flight combat aircraft 1945

During the second half of 1942, extra-terrestrial incursions into Earth's atmosphere increased considerably. This was due to both a growing interest in Earth affairs and a response to diplomatic overtures by both the Axis and Allies. In 1937, a number of emissaries arrived on Earth and negotiated the so-called Marax Protocols (named after the chief extra-terrestrial negotiator). The protocols formalised relations between Earth's major powers and a number of extra-terrestrial species. This included a pledge of no direct interference in Earth conflicts, although paving the way for exchanges of materiel and technology, as well as basing agreements.

Wartime expediency saw attempts by Earth's alliances to renegotiate the terms of the protocols, some nations attempting to do so unilaterally. The Japanese, in particular, sought increased supplies of technology from both the

K'lmar and Yarl. Heavy-handed Japanese negotiations ultimately alienated the latter and pushed them into pro-Allied neutrality by the end of 1944.

S Flight was the principal British organisation tasked with maintaining diplomatic relations with extra-terrestrials. S flight personnel conducted negotiations at facilities in Western Scotland, Australia and a joint Anglo-French facility in Antarctica. Fears persisted that certain species may take advantage of the protocols to gather intelligence to be traded with Axis governments. As a result, an increasingly important role for C Flight became efforts to detect extra-terrestrial incursions into British airspace. Initially, this relied on mystics and psychics attuned to off off-world beings. In May 1943, devices jointly developed with DExNA entered production that enabled the atmospheric disruption caused by space craft drives to be detected.

Despite failed and frequent clumsy human diplomacy, extra-terrestrials adhered to protocols and no significant breaches are known to have occurred. The experience gained by APIB formed the basis of the on-going multinational Operation Sky Cage in Europe and North Africa. Particularly important was the technology received from the Yarl and other races following a breakdown of relations with the Axis. Japanese intransigence in meeting the demands of off-world species had been particularly damaging, while Italy had been a lynch pin for diplomatic efforts in Europe that was were lost following their surrender in 1943.[33] Of the major races, only the militaristic, semi-aquatic *K'lmar* and their allies maintained significant ties to Germany after February 1944.

---

[33] Many of the Italian Navy's Caelus Extra Terrestrial Diplomatic Team defected to DExNA in 1943.

The result of the break down in relations between the Axis and extra-terrestrials was a growing exchange of technology for resources with the Allies. This was not altruistic, as a number of races sought to leverage support from any quarter due to growing instability on the fringes of the Milky Way. Furthermore, the exact nature of the resources offered by organisations such as APIB, DExNA and the French Airforce's Jade Unit remain highly classified.

Almost certainly, the movement of humans, possibly off-world was involved, as well as a tacit agreement to turn a blind eye to certain extra-terrestrial activities on Earth. In regard to dealings with extra-terrestrials, the Western Allies considerably lagged behind the USSR. During 1931 and 1932, the Soviets had traded population and artefacts recovered from the site of the Tunguska event. Similarly, both the IJA's Fūten organisation and the SS's Black Sun unit had traded 'undesirables' and conducted exchanges of 'personnel' during the war.

The benefit to APIB's capabilities from dealings with extra-terrestrials was considerable. In 1945 the Yarl provided a specialist device for fitting to a Meteor aircraft that would home in on emissions from alien craft in the upper atmosphere. A number of war spheres were also supplied to both the Britain and the USA. They utilised a number of off off-world technologies, such as disruptive electromagnetic fields and advanced propulsion. These were tested in the skies above Europe, including trials against both RAF and US 8th AF bomber formations. Operational security was aided by the fabrication of confusing reports alleging the existence of hi-tech enemy aircraft nicknamed 'foo-fighters'. Rumours persist of a number of encounters with German war saucers over the Baltic in the closing weeks of the war and after, but these remain unsubstantiated. The breakdown in relations between the Yarl and pro-Soviet Thermarae resulted in further exchanges in 1954 and 1967.

While supporting S Flight's operations in relation to extra-terrestrials, C Flight was also tasked with countering Earth-based opponents. It was initially estimated that this threat would primarily consist of the flying creatures employed by NZL and SS.Kp.K. EAWAC utilised a number of means, including infiltration by Excalibur operatives, to monitor the activities of both groups. In November 1941, a report to EWE leadership estimated that within two years, the creatures would be combat combat-ready.

The German flying creature programme had, in fact, been accelerated due to fears of dragons being employed by the Allies. Ironically, the collapse of the Myrddin Project fueled this further as the Ahnenerbe believed the project to be ongoing, but so effectively shielded that German seers were unable to penetrate the defensive wards.[34] It has since been theorised that the supposed wards were, in fact misidentified magical energies given off by a number of artefacts moved into Wales for security reasons at the outbreak of the war.[35] In an effort to gather intelligence about the supposed British Dragon programme, a joint Ahnenerbe–Mer mission was launched in January 1941. The force was ambushed soon after landing on the Pembrokeshire coast by an RMOWU detachment, acting on intelligence supplied pro-Allied Mers in the Irish Sea.

The result of rising German paranoia was enhancement of existing flying were-creatures and further experimentation. Often, this utilised knowledge gained from

---

[34] This was also tacit recognition of the growing gap between Allied and access remote viewing capabilities.

[35] Arthur's crown and Beowulf's warhammer being among them.

Vichy French scientists who had been employed by Sapphire prior to the French surrender. A number of Valkyries were also recruited to fill the ranks of SS.Kp.K in return for mystical artefacts such as the great spear of Ullr. NZL's airborne weres were the first creatures to reach combat trials, but the results were disappointing. Like their ground ground-based counterparts in 1940, they were too vulnerable to large large-caliber calibre gunfire, particularly the cannons that were increasingly common on fighter aircraft.

Following a small number of limited operations on the Eastern Front (primarily against lone reconnaissance aircraft), NZL ceased frontline operations by its creatures in July 1943. This was followed by SS.Kp.K in November. From this point, the creatures of both formations were deployed to protect facilities in remote parts of Germany that were associated with occult operations. SS.Kp.K airborne formations provided security for the *Die Glocke* facilities in Norway during 1944, as well as escorts to visiting *K'lmar* War craft.[36] A small detachment of winged- weres and Valkyries was also assigned to Operation *Gebirgswächter* on counter-partisan operations. This unit was withdrawn to Austria in January 1945.

In conjunction with Sapphire, C Flight had prepared a number of strategies to counter the anticipated threat posed the airborne units of NZL and SS.Kp.K. By May 1943, a considerable quantity of silver ammunition had been stockpiled and preparations made to acquire fighter aircraft from storage. In December 1944, much of this ammunition was hastily deployed by the OOE to Yugoslav Chetnik groups and Italian Partisans. The reasons for this remain

---

[36] See Chapter 2 'Hammer of a God'

unclear, although EWE seers had reported the deployment of a Soviet lycan- unit to Croatia some weeks before. APIB recognized recognised that the most effective counter to airborne creatures were similar beings. As a result, a coven led by members of the Northern Sabbat was established under APIB command in the Great Lakes region of Canada, as part of Operation Red- Bat.

Working closely with the shaman of the Huron, Wendat and Algonquin peoples, the Red-Bat coven was to ascertain the feasibility of co-operating with the airborne spirit entities of the region. Agreement was reached with a number of entities for defensive operations in North America but negotiations concerning European operations were unsuccessful and ceased in May 1942. The final report to the Northern Sabbat concluded:

> Few entities have been encountered of with such power, determination and diplomatic skill. We were persistently led down avenues of negotiation that proved to be dead ends or distractions. The defensive agreements we have reached are, in fact, of little value as it is believed that entities acknowledged by all North American cultures remain ever vigilant in any case. Their unity gives them a further, immutable strength. What little we have gained these past months is further understanding of their pre-human contacts with Old World fay [sic.] and mers, although how much of this is fact and not carefully woven deception remains unclear.

In 1943, Red-Bat was transferred to the Anglo-US Operation Prairie Emperor in an effort to bind the Thunderbird entities of the Plains Indians. Again unsuccessful, the coven was redeployed that December to British Columbia. Its new mission was to monitor the activities of the IJN's *Yōkai* organisation in the North Pacific.

The final component of APIB's plans to counter the threat of airborne creatures was the deployment of elementals. EWE had been reluctant to operate alongside such creatures since the incident aboard the airship R101 in October 1930. This had resulted in the craft's destruction, the event being attributed to adverse weather conditions. Despite this, it was increasingly apparent that elementals were potentially useful. At the very least their study was necessary to develop counters in the event of such beings utilised by the enemy. A joint EWE-APIB-ICG elemental warfare unit, codenamed Monolith, was established in 1940 with the aim of summoning, binding and deploying elementals. From June 1940, Monolith also included French Sapphire teams.

Elementals proved extremely difficult to control, even after the addition of coven groups assigned to Operation Charon. It was soon discovered that once an elemental broke its binding enchantments (a not uncommon event) they had a tendency to rapidly expend their energy and such events could, in many cases, be dismissed as freak natural occurrences. This aided operational security. In the winter of 1941, a number of live tests were conducted on unsuspecting aircraft and crews over the North Sea in the winter of 1940-41. These tests led to the loss of a number of RAF and Royal Navy personnel, officially to 'unknown causes' or, if convenient, 'enemy action'. Despite this, the losses demonstrated the viability of the concept. From January 1942 until November 1945, Monolith expanded trials to the China, India and Pacific theatres under Operation Southern Storm.

The tests of 1940-41, while valuable in demonstrating the potential capability of elementals in air warfare, did little to enhance the understanding of such beings. Intriguingly, EWE seers had breached the wards guarding the Nazis' elemental programmes in 1938. Yet, the intelligence gained had provided little tangible benefit. As was often the case in the mystical operations of the Third Reich, sometimes scarce resources were scattered between organisations. The situation improved marginally in August 1939 when the SS stood down its elemental warfare research department. This left separate and competing programmes in the Luftwaffe, Kriegsmarine, Wehrmacht and Thule Society. The latter maintained no fewer than three separate projects. Of them all, it was the project under the Luftwaffe's Walküre that showed the most promise. The greatest success of this programme was in June 1944 when its elementals created a storm as part of an attempt to halt Allied operations in Normandy.

Most important for developing British elemental warfare capabilities was the defection of a CBB coven of Siberian Shaman through northern Persia in 1942. The coven had been part of Operation Ice Bolt, a Soviet effort to manipulate weather patterns during the winter of 1941. Although successful, the coven had come to the attention of the NKVD and had evaded capture before crossing into British territory by creating a sudden blizzard. The defection was a propaganda coup and they were taken to India for debriefing by Southern Storm's leading elementalist, Rajwant Gadkari.

Born in Mysore in 1907, Gadkari was a powerful mystic who had been courted by radical Indian Nationalists due to both her power and ruthlessness. In 1924, Gadkari had reportedly summoned an elemental that had destroyed a party of bandits in the Khyber Pass and had worked alongside the British as part of Operation Artemis. This employment had continued through other clandestine mystic operations, including incursions into Afghanistan, China and Nepal. In 1931, Gadkari was recruited by the ICG and participated in a number of operations in India, Burma and in Southern China. This included leading a team that wiped out a Yeti colony in retaliation for the kidnapping of an AREBaC representative, cementing her reputation for brutality. It was this brutality that would enable the British to capitalise on the defection of the Soviet coven.

Within 24 hours of the Gadkari Gadkari-led interrogation commencing, all six members of the former Soviet coven were dead. EWE was outraged: not only had the interrogation taken place without their consent, but six potentially valuable mystics had been killed. Chris Turton, the ICG's liaison to Southern Storm, took a different view and wrote to his APIB counter part.

> The fact is that for the loss of six 'gifted' yak herders we now have the knowledge to expand defensive and offensive operations through Monolith. I propose that she [Gadkari] remain in theatre until after the next monsoon season and then deploy to North Africa to support offensive operations. It is there and in Europe that the real business of this war is being conducted. Let EWE bleat. We now have a war war-winning asset.

Gadkari ultimately left Southern Storm in May 1943 and commenced trials with APIB's M and C Flights that September. EWE had effectively withdrawn from Monolith that August, leaving only a small team of observers. Officially, this was to enable EWE to focus on its marine leviathan projects.[37] This was symptomatic of two fundamental changes in Britain's esoteric warfare apparatus. EWE, like many organisations, was experiencing a significant deficiency of mystics, seers and similar individuals. Perhaps more significantly, there were again growing divisions between Britain's occult warfare organisations.

Turton's appraisal of Gadkari's capabilities soon proved to be optimistic. Efforts to employ elementals in Italy during January 1944 were countered by the Abwehr's Hexenzirkel Witzel. This was followed by the successful deployment of an SS Wotan detachment to terminate the group of elementalists operating with Italian partisans. Monolith also proved only marginally effective in countering Walküre's use of elementals in activities to disrupt the Allied landings in Normandy. German capabilities had been enhanced through the capture of extra-terrestrial technology of *Thermarae* origin that had been captured from the Soviets in 1942. This was a rare instance in which off-world technology was effectively used to enhance mystical operations, it being likely that the disruption to the Normandy campaign may have been even greater had if not for Monolith.

In November 1944 Monolith mystics participated in a number of Bomber Command operations over Germany in modified Mosquitos. This was an effort to enhance bombing using fire elementals, but the results were indecisive. In total, eight so so-called Hades operations were mounted. Their effectiveness, or lack thereof, can be measured by the fact that there is no evidence the Germans even detected the

---

[37] See Chapter 8 'Marine Leviathans'

deployment of elementals. In part, this vindicated Huxley's assertions of 1940 that an effective defense defence would prevent the augmentation of bombing operations by mystical means. By 1945, however, something more fundamental was apparent to all those involved in occult warfare: the technology of war had surpassed the capabilities of mystics and the occult. It was a gap that would widen further.

Chapter 8

Marine Leviathans

The occupation of Norway brought Germany many strategic advantages. One of the most significant was easy access to the breeding grounds of sea serpents and other marine leviathans that stretched from Norway to Greenland. A number of species could be found in this region, but of particular interest to the Nazis were the so-called seedrache, or sea dragons. These were particularly aggressive sea serpents suited to warfare and the sinking of naval vessels.

Unbeknownst to the allies O.Abt.K had scored a major success in preliminary efforts to tame a seedrache even before the fall of Norway. This had been used to provide intelligence of the movements of the British aircraft carrier HMS Glorious, leading to her sinking during the evacuation of British forces from Norway in 1940. This had been a rude awakening for those tasked with planning Britain's occult warfare strategy. A string of German diplomatic blunders had ensured the neutrality of most Mer tribes. These were the aquatic fae races who controlled the sea serpents and other creatures that the Nazis sought to utilise.[38]

The shock of the sinking of the Glorious was twofold. The Nazis had been able to deploy a marine leviathan of

---

[38] While many tribes remained neutral, a handful supported the Allied cause. Fewer supported the Axis. Despite those pro-German Mers were instrumental in the attack on Scapa Flow of October 1939, in which the battle cruiser HMS Royal Oak was sunk.

some description in a frontline role, and, of most concern, there was little indication of its type or capabilities. Indeed, only a chance sighting report by a Royal Navy lookout and a trickle of intelligence from Mers associated with Operation Tidal Wave gave any indication of what had happened. As it was, EWE had little option but to advise the Royal Navy to avoid the area least they were heading into a trap. The result was a large number of casualties caused by a disjointed rescue operation, in which even Merfolk allied to the British were reluctant to take part. They, too, were concerned, an ill omen for British plans.

The leading authority on German efforts to tame, train and deploy a seedrache was a Frenchman assigned to the Atlantic section of the French Navy's Ruby unit. The team had been set up in 1887 in response to encounters with unusually large reptilians in the jungles and swamps of France's African colonies. Sieur Baudin had been transferred to the unit in 1922. This followed a deployment to central Africa, where he encountered the creature known to locals as *Mokele-mbembe*.

An occultist since the horrors of the trenches Baudin recognised that *Mokele-mbembe* was not a creature of a mystic realm, but one of mortal flesh and blood. This was a radical, albeit correct departure at a time when there was a resurgence of mystical societies and efforts to militarise the occult and supernatural in all of their forms. The no-nonsense approach to the prehistoric survivor, combined with a sensitivity to the paranormal, enabled Baudin to progress quickly and gain access to some of the leading pseudo-scientists and practitioners of magick, a discipline of magic championed by the British occultist Aleister Crowley

(Crowley and Baudin briefly met at a Qaballa ritual in Paris during 1914). Baudin, in co-operation with the Russian occultist Lazar Abaza, became interested in the concept of the sea serpents of legend being aspects of the elemental force of water.

In 1924, Baudin and Lazar launched an investigation of Loch Ness. Their breakthrough would be achieved through using West African rituals to contact and then summon the creature that frequented the loch. This strategy was employed according to Abaza's theory that the *Mokele-mbembe*, while not itself magical, evaded regular contact through blessings delivered the shamans of the region. If their magic could hide such a creature, then surely they could reveal it. The value of being able to counter magical invisibility in wartime would be incalculable.

The creature was summoned to the North Sea. Here Baudin and Abaza were able to study the creature, with its co-operation, and make a series of discoveries that would have significant consequences in wartime if the creatures could be deployed as weapons. Not least of these discoveries was that the creature and others of its kind were not wholly corporeal, limiting the ability of sonar or other technology to detect them. Indeed, even mystical methods of viewing were rendered partly ineffective by their forms. By sheer chance the creature's ability to evade detection appeared to be most vulnerable to the magics practice in parts of West Africa. Another finding of the study was that as a species few of the creatures were alike.

In 1939 there would have been no doubt that the information gained from the investigation would have been shared with the British. Conversely, during the 1920s, it remained unclear who the next opponent would be. The seers employed in the intelligence detachments of the Emerald teams pointed towards a future conflict with Germany. Despite this, the alliance between Britain and France during the Great War had for many been an aberration. This was particularly true for those conservative elements who practised the occult. It was, they reasoned, far better to plan for war with either Germany or Britain, rather than show their hand. The French also had reason to be confident because, while the secrets of Atlantis were being dissected by British and others, the zoological archives had been removed en masse to Emerald's archives at Carnac. It was apparent that Atlantis had struggled for millennia to bend the creatures to their will and ultimately failed, possibly leading to a war that resulted in the destruction of their whole civilisation.

With no knowledge from the archives held in France, while and lacking the understanding gained by Baudin and Abaza, the British knew little of the creatures that Germans would call *seedrache*. Operation Tidal Wave had focused on the Mer tribes who attended their needs, rather than the creatures themselves. It was only through the efforts of missions such as those of Operation Tidal Wave that EWE began to fully comprehend the significance of the creatures. Seen as little more than novelty beasts, it only slowly became apparent evident to the British and others that they possessed significant military potential. Conversely, the *Ahnenerbe* and O.Abt.K began to take an interest in the creatures as soon as it became apparent that Germany was preparing to fight an undersea war. German efforts to harness the power of the creatures was, like the British and France, hampered by rivalry. The *Ahnenerbe* had the fullest knowledge of the creatures, having mounted an expedition to Lake Baikal in 1934. The *Ahnenerbe* had also gleaned understanding from expeditions to Java and Manchuria, alongside access to limited amounts of knowledge from the Japanese.

While the *Ahnenerbe* possessed information, O.Abt.K had been more proactive, seeking to contact the creatures much as Baudin and Lazar had done. In 1938, as part of a practice operation for the employment of raider vessels against British shipping, the Kriegsmarine despatched a coven of Bavarian witches aboard a merchant vessel to the mid-Atlantic. The vessel successfully evaded detection due in part to the imprinting of a shrouding sigil on the hull that deceived EWE seers. More importantly, the runesmith Sven Kilbom was assigned to the vessel. Kilbom specialised in runes derived from Hyperborean sources and was able to summon and bind a creature. This would be the only successful binding of a seedrache by German forces by the time of the Norwegian campaign. A second attempt in the following month to cast the runes resulted in the mental breakdown of Kilbom and the loss of the vessel with all its crew. The death of so many mystics in one event proved devastating to those remotely sensing the event in Hamburg, causing further damage to the organisation. It was an event from which the organisation would never fully recover. Further damage would be done in 1944. Mers under the direction of DExNA recovered many of the ship's artefacts, including an Assyrian Grimoire, from the ocean floor.

Although the British lacked knowledge of the creatures studied by Baudin, enough information had emerged for the British to view him as an expert of such matters. With the enemy clearly Germany, a nation pursuing their own attempts to weaponise the creatures, the French now opened the relevant archives to the British. To their horror, EWE's leadership discovered that the French knew far more about the beast residing in a Scottish loch than the British themselves. In conjunction with Baudin and personnel from various Emerald and Ruby detachments, it became apparent to EWE that German occultists had developed a means to at least partially control a sea serpent. The question was how this had been achieved as the significant Mer tribes within the region were considered to be under British influence and their menageries secure. Eventually, locating the creature by a combination of pendulum divination and scrying was almost a certainty, the question was how long and how much damage could it inflict until countered.

While the divination effort aimed at the North Sea gathered pace, Baudin began building an intelligence picture of German *seedrache* operations. In the long term, this would prepare a counter to future activities. It would also better prepare EWE to counter the current threat and possibly determine its extent. Attention was focused on the Baltic and areas on the German and Dutch North Sea coast where Tidal Wave teams had encountered the most German activity. Of particular value were the reports concerning the failed attempt by O.Abt.K to obtain a creature from the Merfolk. This particular beast was bred for war, its bony collar and horns forming a brutally effective ram. It was also likely to possess acoustic detection capabilities far in excess of contemporary sonar systems. Reported by the Merfolk of the Skagerrak as being notoriously temperamental and hard to tame, the logical conclusion was that O.Abt.K had been preparing the creature for years, suggesting an allied intelligence failure of immense proportions. Yet where were other attacks, or pressingly when would they occur?

The breakthrough came in early July when an observer aboard a Hudson of the RAF's Coastal Command reported what appeared to be a surfaced U-boat a mile from the Norfolk coast. The aircraft dived to attack but, despite the fading twilight, the crew reported:

> a long serpent-like creature, 30 to 40 feet long, with spines and plate-like structures. It seemed to propel itself through the water by flexing its body left to right in a wave-like motion.

The crew who observed the creature were immediately grounded due 'psychological stress brought on by extended operations' and hastily debriefed by EWE investigators. This, combined with knowledge gained from a bestiary recovered from a sunken Atlantean colony in the Persian Gulf, confirmed that O.Abt.K had indeed found a creature suited for attack. It was, however, a creature that could only be controlled by Hyperborean magic.

Infiltration of German occult groups had revealed the loss of Kilbom in 1938 and slowly the pieces of the jigsaw fell into place. Kilbom had bound only one creature, maybe two, as any greater number would have been noticed. It was also correctly deduced that

    a)   the operation against HMS Glorious in June 1940 was the first operational use

b) that the creature had been deployed on low-key combat operations to test the limits of the control over the creature.

Casualties inflicted by the creature, both supposed and confirmed, would be counted as 'loses to enemy mines'. The British turned to Baudin for a solution. His proposal was to break the enchantments that bound the creature and rebind it to the allies. The mission was given the codename Operation Shetland. It was scheduled for Autumn 1940.

The challenge for the Shetland planners was knowing where and when the *seedrache* would operate so that Baudin could strike. This was a problem that would limit the occult operations of all nations during the war. Practitioners of magic were simply too few in number to have enough available for general deployment, and training could only enhance existing abilities present an individual, not create them. The colonial empires of Britain and France gave the Allies a significantly larger pool of such resources to draw on, but it was nonetheless limited. What was needed was something sufficient to draw the attention of the O.Abt.K's planners and prompt the deployment of the seedrache.

Since the sinking of the Glorious, the *seedrache's* mission had gone beyond reconnaissance, but the sinkings of merchant ships from Britain's east coast convoys were trials only. Worryingly for O.Abt.K these trials had demonstrated that the creature had yet to be fully tamed and the introduction of this potentially war-changing weapon was delayed. The unit's mystics had correctly identified that Hyperborean magic was the best way to fully bind the creature, but the Thule Society had a near monopoly on this school of magic in the Third Reich. Hitler's favoured astrologers and mystics were drawn from the society and they carefully guarded its secrets. The result was that the Nazis remained unwilling to commit the creature and it ventured outside the fjords rarely. It seemed to the Shetland planners that they needed significant bait to force the deployment of the *seedrache* against a target of their choosing. The answer was proposed by Arcano-archaeologist Devlin Firth.

Firth had been cross-attached to the Shetland team from APIB's Project Myrddin . An Oxford graduate, Firth had undertaken Arcano-archaeological surveys of the North American Eastern Seaboard in the late 1920s. His conclusions had been considered too outlandish even by EWE. Firth may have languished in obscurity but for a chance meeting with Air Marshal Hugh Dowding at a séance. In the Air Marshal Firth had found an influential backer. In particular, Dowding had been impressed by Firth's theories about the emigration of Fae settlers across the Atlantic from Wales at the end of the forth century. Firth had also came to the attention of DExNA due to his proposal that the fae had not only returned to their homeland but did so to reactivate certain gateways of a non-terrestrial origin. In 1938 Dowding had inducted Firth into Myrddin and, following the French surrender, assigned him as a liaison to EWE.

Firth was initially considered to be something of a maverick. He received an icy reception due to his views of extra-terrestrial entities and their relationship with those of Earth. Firth was in many ways the victim of a conservative dogma that would lead to the decline of Western European dominance in occult warfare in the post-war period. Despite such views, it rapidly became apparent that Firth possessed a razor-sharp mind. His theories about the extra-terrestrial origins of Mer-folk deities facilitated major breakthroughs in diplomacy with tribes residing in Greenland. Firth thus found himself assigned to the Shetland team in the hope that he could bring a fresh perspective to the problem of ensnaring the *seedrache*. In typical fashion, Firth proposed a solution that combined the mystical with the extra-terrestrial.

It had long been clear that relations between the various occult organisations of Nazi Germanys were strained. Thus Firth reasoned that the most effective bait to draw the attention of O.Abt.K would be an artefact sought by a rival Nazis organisation, but also one considered expendable to the Allied war effort. The artefact selected was the so-called Baffin Object. This was an extra-terrestrial craft that came down on Baffin Island in 1908, it being identified in 1963 as a class of inter-system courier ship. Intriguingly, Innuit fishermen reported seeing it rise from the sea, before being struck by a 'rod of green light' from above. It subsequently crashed on Baffin Island and was covertly salvaged four months later. EWE adopted its regular usual ambiguous approach to extra-terrestrial technology, with the result and that it languished unstudied in a secure facility. An Imperial German Naval Air Service *Walküre* (Valkyrie) Team took an interest in reports surrounding the artefact. German mystics penetrated the wards that should have screened it and were able to deduce much about the craft. Ambitious plans to retrieve it were not implemented due to the end of hostilities in 1918. Information surrounding the object was eventually passed down to the rejuvenated *Walküre* organisation in 1933, which was then under the newly created Luftwaffe.

Walküre immediately set to work on trying to establish the whereabouts of the craft. This was prevented by measures adopted by EWE to counter hostile scrying and remote viewing efforts. These include runic wards and Hyperborean enchantments. Desperate for information about the object, *Walküre's* leadership was also anxious to take a lead over its rivals. The result was an ineptly executed effort at infiltrating amongst other organisations the *Ahnenerbe, S.S. Bataillon de Nachtwanderer* (BdN) and O.Abt.K. The result outcome was a brief and somewhat bloody civil war fought between Nazis Germany's military occultists, cementing the mistrust that would characterise Nazis occult operations throughout the war. More importantly for Operation Shetland, O.Abt.K's leaders now knew *Walküre* sought the Baffin artefact. As with EWE, it was very much the view of O.Abt.K's leadership that research into such extra-terrestrials was a dead end. In the atmosphere of bitter rivalry that characterised the occult organisations of Nazis Germany, the destruction of the Baffin Object thus became more important than its possession.

The bait was identified and it was now time to place it in the trap. A coven was established to increase warding spells at the subterranean storage facility used to store the Baffin artefact. Simultaneously, a small convoy was built up nearby and three days later, a merchant vessel was screened by numerous runes and sigils. The consequence was the creation of two voids of mystical output in close proximity, and the fact that one was a merchant vessel in particular would inevitably attracted the attention of O.Abt.K.. Two days after efforts to breach the British screening efforts were detected, two Athabaskan shaman conducted a protection ritual at the facility. Having only limited access to such branches of magic it was known the Germans would take some days to counter this. Simultaneously, Allied operatives arranged for the murder of key survivors of the original *Walküre* team from 1917. This It was an operation that would see the first employment of a British pyrotechnic entity within German borders.

The murder of former operatives further drew the attention of *Walküre* to both the objects' supposed location and their imminent removal. By now each of O.Abt.K and *Walküre* had drawn the conclusion intended by Firth: the Baffin object was to be moved by sea and that the British intended to deploy it operationally in the future. O.Abt.K could thwart the perceived British intention and deprive *Walküre* of its prize in one operation. In different circumstances, a conventional option would have been considered, but given intensive British mystical activities, this was swiftly ruled out.

On September 19 a meeting of the inner council of the O.Abt.K leadership and its senior mystics approved the deployment of the *seedrache* as 'the optimal and sensible solution to the problem of the artefact'. Klaudia Schwarz, a pagan priestess operating with O.Abt.K, noted post-war that

> it was as if the war with Britain was over and it was time to finish the real enemy. There were high hopes for the *seedrache* and we were all drunk on optimism

despite the problems we were having. It was a chance for us to gain dominance ready for the future occult struggle within Nazis Germany

Intelligence gained from Operation Tidal Wave revealed to British planners that the *seedrache* was to be prepared for rapid deployment for an estimated window of 23 to September 30 1940. This was a major success as it was the intention to simulate a departure of approximately September 25. In fact,

The convoy would be carrying nothing more than coal and one other cargo that was unknown to the crews, namely Baudin, Abaza and the team of mystics that would break the binding magics and then cast their own enchantments. Through sighting reports from Mer tribes in Norway and intensive pendulum divination, the *seedrache's* progress was tracked across the North Sea and it was estimated that contact would be made near the mouth of Thames. On September 26 Baudin and his team began the enchantments that would slowly begin to break down the magic binding the *seedrache*. The aim was to achieve a slow erosion of the magic so that new binding spells could be phased in, rather than a rapid collapse in which the creature would revert to its feral, uncontrolled state. It was a plan that would no doubt have succeeded if German binding efforts had been fully effective. Against only a partially bound creature, however, even the cautious approach selected by Baudin would have rapid and dramatic consequences.

The sudden breaking of the binding magic was first detected by a Peruvian seer assigned to Baudin's team. Attempting to reach out psychically to the *seedrache* just as the binding spells collapsed, the result was like a small bomb going off within his head. The mystics looked on in horror as the seer collapsed, blood seeping from his nose, eyes and ears. Rolling on the floor in agony, he was just able to rasp in his broken English that the creature was unbound. An experienced mystic, Abaza ordered a switch to their ownother binding spells, but against the renewed consciousness of the now free seedrache it was like trying to punch through a brick wall.

The circle of mystics aboard the vessel was now broken as several of them rushed to the aid of the now-dead seer. Without the mystical circle, their presence was plain to the enraged leviathan that lay a little over one mile away, no doubt already crashing through the sea towards them. They had not been the ones to bind the beast, but it was now free and anxious to lash out at the nearest prey. Physiologically in part composed of magical energy, the awakening of the seedrache's psyche triggered a wave of mystical forces that manifested on the surface as boiling water. An alert lookout aboard an escorting destroyer shouted a warning and the vessel's captain immediately ordered full speed in an attempt to engage what he believed to be a U-boat close to the surface. His aggressive action, in the best traditions of the Royal Navy, would place the vessel directly between the *seedrache* and the merchant vessel. Officially the destroyer would be recorded as lost to enemy torpedoes: as three torpedo wakes were being reported on its port side moments before impact. EWE analysts would deduce these to be the tips of the seedrache's horns breaking the water as the central wake was stated to be some distance ahead of the others. Baudin and Abaza both reported that afterwards the creature, its rage sated, retired to the chill grey waters of the North Sea.

According to EWE's initial analysis, Operation Shetland was a failure. The Allies had not gained control of the *seedrache*. Furthermore, through studying the operation, O.Abt.K and similar Nazis organisations could have potentially gained valuable insights into British occult operations, particularly the employment of Athabaskan Shaman and the sigils used to screen the merchant vessel. These fears proved unfounded and it was suspected that the warding had been so efficient that the German mystics had simply been unable to identify the array of mystical strategies employed against them. It was only after the war that the truth emerged.

The reason for Operation Shetland's failure was the ineffective binding of the *seedrache*. This had long been known to by O.Abt.K and it was this that led to the German conclusion that the creature had broken free of the binding due to its own efforts, not British interference. Nonetheless, even in 1940, it was apparent that for the loss of a World War I vintage destroyer, EWE had been able to deprive Germany of a marine leviathan, while its warding activities had proved effective in preventing German viewing efforts in the deception phase of the operation. Through Operation Tidal Wave, the British could also monitor further German efforts to utilise creatures at sea. Despite their failure to bind the creature during Operation Shetland, both Baudin and Abaza continued to work with Allies to gain control of leviathans of various kinds.

It was increasingly evident that EWE's emphasis on mysticism had caused it to fall behind its rivals in key areas.

Shetland demonstrated this to be particularly true in the arena of marine leviathans. British research had focused on sea serpents, but analysis of bestiaries retrieved from Atlantis had allowed the French Navy's Ruby unit to identify, seek out and ultimately study an array of marine leviathans. Most of these creatures dwelt within the depths of Atlantic, Arctic and Pacific regions. Of particular value to EWE was a French analysis of Italian efforts to bind marine leviathans in the eastern Mediterranean. It seemed that EWE had significantly underestimated the capabilities of the Italian Navy's Trident Unit, having believed it to be primarily focused on mystical activities. Instead it appeared that by 1942, it would be able to deploy three marine leviathans, two of which would be in the Red Sea.[39]

Trident had also began the process of reviving an unknown number of prehistoric creatures, including reptilians, that had been placed in suspended animation during the fall of Atlantis. Although behind the three major Axis powers in this field, a report issued by EWE's M Office concluded that there were grounds for optimism:

1. Marine leviathans could not be easily bound and employed
2. Britain's conventional naval forces could contest Axis naval ambitions
3. Italy's capabilities were split between two seas

The report also noted that the majority of France's occultists had joined the Free French. Significantly these French occult

---

[39] This was a double failure on the part of Allied intelligence, as they failed to discover until 1943 that Trident was infact an offshoot of Operation Lilith. See Chapter 1 'Spirit and Beast Warfare'.

forces and other units were building up in Africa as part of Operation Blood Raven. This would allow the allies to fully exploit the occult resources of the continent, giving them a tremendous mystical reserve. Despite this, the decision was made to deploy 40% of the Ruby and Emerald units' manpower strength to Britain. The objective was to begin a campaign with the aims of:

1. bringing marine leviathans' under British control
2. limiting Axis capabilities to challenge conventional Allied naval forces
3. protecting the vital North Atlantic convoy routes

Expeditions were immediately mounted into the northern marine leviathan breeding grounds with the goal of achieving the first aim.

The initial burst of Anglo-French co-operation in the field of occult activity waned. The French political establishment contained many Anglo-phobes while occultists tended to be traditionalists, and perceiving the British were to be the traditional enemy of France. The mistrust of Britain's ambitions towards France's occult capabilities was not without foundation. EWE, in particular, had long sought to gain access to the mystical knowledge within the French colonial Empire. It is well documented that many in the organisation had viewed co-operation as an opportunity to gain control under the guise of allied unity. Mortal greed and jealousy had as ever outdone the possibilities offered by the mystical and occult.

Although reduced, Anglo-French co-operation never fully ceased. In addition, mystics from all nations had gained a reputation as freelancers. Free French 'observers' (invariably from Ruby teams) made numerous journeys over northern seas in RAF Coastal Command flying boats. More than one crew would be bewildered by the various sigils and summoning symbols they would find within their aircraft. March 1941 would see a particularly ambitious joint Ruby-EWE operation aimed at co-operating with Mers to locate the breeding grounds of Kraken. Deployed 15 miles west of Hamnöya by a submarine of the Royal Netherlands Navy, the team consisted of two members of RMOWU, a Ruby operative and a Free-French advisor to Operation Tidal Wave. Ten minutes after launching their kayaks, the team were almost detected by a Luftwaffe Ar-196 sea plane that was patrolling the area. Soon after, the team rendezvoused with a local Mer delegation. From here, the team was taken down to a nearby Mer settlement and a meeting with the tribe's 'Keeper of Beasts'.

In an agreement negotiated as part of Operation Tidal Wave, the team offered the ruling chieftain a defensive pact. This was accepted and modelled on those agreed with other tribes. A number of ancient artefacts were also presented. These had been request by the Mers and had been retrieved by the Dutch from ruins off of the coast of Java in 1938. In return, the Mers guided the team to the location of the kraken breeding grounds and participated in a joint binding of a mature kraken. The beast was given the codename Lacerater. This creature would be responsible for the destruction of a number of Axis naval craft and marine leviathans. The former would include a number of deep ocean exploration U-boats derived from off-world *K'lmar* technology.

Date	Allied	German	Italian
September 1939	0	1	
May 1940 (Fall of France)	0	1	1
December 1941 (Pearl Harbour)	4	2	3
December 1942	5	4	3
December 1943	6	3	2★
June 1944 (D–Day)	6	3	
May 1945 (VE Day)	7	2	
★bound into German service following seizure of Trident headquarters at Venice			

Figure 12: active marine Leviathans available for operations in Atlantic and Arctic waters,1939 to 1945.

Lacerater was one of a number of marine leviathans bound by the Allies with the intention of countering those of the Axis powers. An analysis of this strategy was conducted by M Office in 1946 and determined that:

The Arctic convoy routes were the main theatre in which the Leviathans leviathans of the Allied powers were deployed. In the period August 1941 to May 1945, 1,400 merchant ships carried supplies to the USSR. It is estimated that only three merchants and three escorts were attacked by hostile leviathans. The potential lethality of these attacks is demonstrated by the fact that five of the vessels were lost. Despite these losses it remains apparent that only six attacks were conducted, even though convoy routes to the USSR passed through the heart of the marine leviathan breeding grounds accessible to Nazis Germany.

Forays by Axis leviathans into the North Atlantic were less frequent but often more devastating due to the difficulty of locating them. Almost all of the leviathan's employed by the Nazis were of types that, due to their magical nature, were difficult to detect with sonar and other devices. It was also evident that the way in which the *seedrache* in particular, moved through water further limited the effect of sonar. Finally, certain species, although notably not the *seedrache*, could remain submerged almost indefinitely. This limited the effectiveness of visual searching but also mystical sensing due to the effect of water currents, particularly in the deeper oceans. Fortunately for the Aallies, these constantly submerged species tended to be less aggressive and had fewer adaptations for combat.

Advances in mystical sensing methods, such as pendulum divination, did little to aid detection efforts. This was because such sensing required some localisation to be effective, particularly in regions where magic was particularly strong and liable to give misleading or false readings. Such a region was the North Atlantic, home to some of the most potent primal and elemental energies on the planet. Ultimately, the Allies were able to harness this to aid in the detection of enemy marine leviathans, as it was found that such species tended to avoid areas of the strongest magic.

The effect was first discovered by the Japanese in the summer of 1941, while when attempting to move a large reptilian leviathan to the coast of Indo-China. A British mystical mission in Hong Kong intercepted reports back to an IJN *Yōkai* team located at the creature's layer lair in the Caroline Islands. The information was shared with the French inter-service Emerald mystical intelligence detachment in southern China. This There facilitated followed a powerful efforts by both the British and French teams to mystically observe the operation, which had results of unusual clarity. This was aided by the involvement of Chinese mystics and, significantly, the refusal of the IJN to accept Western occultists could penetrate its own mystical barriers. The British and French teams continued to monitor Japanese efforts to move the creature into position, including its eventual return to the Caroline Islands on December 5 1941.

It was the mystic Margriet Kuyper who identified the reason for the failed deployment. Kuyper, a daughter of Dutch rubber planters, had spent most of her life seeking knowledge of the *Zarlin* culture. The *Zarlin* had thrived in three great cities, supposedly now submerged beneath the Pacific and Indian Oceans.[40] The cities had purportedly been connected by trans-dimensional gateway technology that had collapsed. This contaminated the regions around the cities in non-earthly energies that still continue to leak through in the early twentieth twenty-first century, along with denizens of other realms.

---

[40] The Zarlin gateway system had also enabled the establishment of land colonies in central and western Africa. The misdirection of so called 'Stargate' mythology to Egypt, the Middle East and even the America's in Western cultures remains one the great achievements of occult misinformation.

Kuyper proposed that a fourth, much smaller city had also existed close to Bermuda and that this had caused the anomalies there, while the Devil's Triangle near Japan approximated to the location of one of the larger cities. Kuyper noted that the Japanese had inadvertently been attempting to operate in a region believed to be occupied by the second of great *Zarlin* cities, *Ngo'Ka*. Combine with this knowledge, the British were able to retrace the leviathan's journey back to the Caroline Islands. Clearly, the creature was avoiding areas known to be strong in mystical energy.

By observing the areas of the North Atlantic strongest in mystical energy, M Office were now able to focus sensing activities on more likely areas of hostile marine leviathan activity. The result was a significant reduction in their activities, due to the success of Allied leviathans killing or deterring their Axis counterparts. In late June, both Lacerator and the Sea Serpent codenamed Titan killed two *seedraches* and badly injured three others. Merchant sinkings by marine Leviathans leviathans averaged 2-4 vessels per month in the first half of 1941, loses officially attributed to U-boats. From July, loses amounted to 2 or fewer per month, while the Germans withdrew their remaining leviathans to Norwegian waters. Only a single Italian leviathan, a prehistoric reptile revived by a Trident operation in the Azores, remained in the North Atlantic. The decline in the number of Axis leviathans also allowed Allied leviathans to step up the hunting of U-boats.

With their marine leviathan operations on the verge of collapse, O.Abt.K initiated the Noden Programme. A small number of type VII and type IX U-boats were modified to act as base vessels for covens and teams of mystics in the

North Atlantic. These were given the name of *Zerkel auf See* (Covens at Sea), abbreviated to ZaS.VII or ZaS.IX depending on the original U-boat hulls. The Italian navy began converting two hulls, initially intended to be minelayers. These were not completed by the time of the Italian surrender. The comparable Japanese programme in the Pacific was somewhat more ambitious and developed independently of Noden. Of the allies only the Soviet Navy attempted a similar strategy, as part of Operation Arctic Panther. Both Soviet conversions incorporated elements of extra-terrestrial technology to augment mystic capabilities and remained in service until 1949. The more significant occult resources available to the Western Allies enabled their covens and groups of mystics to operate either remotely, or to be covertly embedded within conventional military forces.

Year	U-boat class					
	Type II	Type VII	Type IX	Type XIV	Type XXI	Type XL*
1942	1T	1	0	0	0	0
1943	0	3	2	0	0	0
1944	0	1	1	1	0	0
1945	0	0	1P	0	1P	1P
Total	1	5	3+1P	1	1P	1P
* Constructed using K'lmar technology; T Trials boat, operated in Baltic; P partial conversion, not completed at wars end						

Figure 13: U-boat conversions carried out under the Noden Programme, 1942 to May 1945

The Noden Programme was intended to support both the leviathan campaign and conventional forces (primarily U-boats). By being within the operational area German mystics were better able to penetrate the defensive wards and enchantments of the Allies. This enhanced intelligence gathering, enabled the covens to support offensive activities and enabled more effective countermeasures against Allied remote sensing activities. The result was that by the end of 1942, German and Italian leviathans were again operating against Allied merchant shipping. Although no more than three were ever at sea at any time the ZaS boats, each carrying two or more covens, were able to restrict the ability of Aallied seers to identify the locations of the leviathans.

Such was the success of the ZaS U-boats that it was proposed to send a number on missions against North America. A joint SS Black Sun/O.Abt.K operation was scheduled for December 1942 utilising a ZaS.IX. This was postponed when the lycans earmarked for the operation, a sabotage mission in New England, were deployed to Russia. In February 1943, a ZaS.VII successfully entered Hudson Bay and its assigned mystics established contact with a powerful Wendigo spirit-elemental.

Known to local tribes as the Howling One, the entity was to have unleashed a potentially devastating sequence of events for upon Canada,, and a yearlong winter in the northern United States. The disturbance created by the awakening of the entity was sensed by a group of First Nation shaman. A joint operation by DExNA and the shaman was conducted to neutralise the German group and placate the Wendigo. Details of the operation remain classified and German documents were seized by a US skinwalker unit in 1945. Rumors persist that soon after the involvement of DExNA, a number of orphanages in the city of Chicago were emptied and their children taken north in a US army convoy. They were not seen again.

The ZaS.VII vessels proved particularly effective at masking both marine leviathan and conventional Kriegsmarine assets. Faced with increasing merchant vessel losses (12 vessels were confirmed sunk by leviathans in August 1942, with other sinkings suspected) the Allies accelerated their leviathan programmes. The US Navy's own marine leviathan unit, known as Ocean-Monarch, achieved its first U-boat kill in January 1941, and its first leviathan kill the following month. In June 1943, Ocean-Monarch scored another success when three of its creatures, aided by Mers and RMOWU teams destroyed the Italian leviathan grounds in the Adriatic. In the waters of the Atlantic and Arctic the ZaS boats were also drawing attention to themselves. This was due to the habit of their mystical screening activities creating voids of mystic energy in areas otherwise strong in it.

Through a combination of leviathan attacks and conventional naval forces, the ZaS boats were hunted down. Conventional forces were frequently guided by mystics covertly assigned to key stations within anti-submarine escort groups. Some successes were also achieved through telekinetic guidance of depth charges. By 1943, losses amongst ZaS vessels mounted and German construction focused on conventional U-boats. Thereafter, sorties into the North Atlantic were sporadic. Trials were conducted in transferring ZaS mystics to conventional U-boats. Conditions in them proved not conducive to the conditions of concentration and harmony required for mystical activities to be effective. The final type of Noden conversion to see service was a unique ZaS.XIV adaptation of a resupply U-boat. Carrying a coven of were-priestesses, it vanished in mysterious circumstances 75 miles southwest of Ireland on its first voyage. The Luftwaffe briefly tested its own airborne version, nicknamed Besenstiel (broomsticks) due to its cargo of witches, in modified Condor aircraft. Officially codenamed Red Horizon, the Besenstiel were ineffective and primarily envisaged as a means to detect allied shipping rather than counter remote sensing activities.

By the spring of 1944, it was apparent Nazis Germany's occult effort at sea had failed. Operations by O.Abt.K, a handful of Mers and the ZaS boats had been unable to significantly counter Allied mystical activities and had only minor influence on the conventional war at sea. The loss of the intelligence war accelerated the demise of the Nazis' marine leviathans. In January 1944, Allied leviathans had hunted down the last of the prehistoric beasts revived by Italy's Trident teams; in March, the surviving German leviathans were withdrawn to Norway. In consequence, on June 6 1944, no leviathan opposed the D-Day invasion armada. Humiliatingly for the *Kreigsmarine*, the main mystic defence against the invasion would come from the Luftwaffe. Of the boats converted by the Noden programme only one, a ZaS.IX, remain. Attempting to reach Japan upon Germany's capitulation, it was intercepted by British leviathans 150 miles east of Madagascar.

Chapter 9

The Road to Medusa

Even though EWE's marine leviathan campaign gained momentum from 1942 there were indications that the organisation was becoming overstretched. Since 1940 EWE's offensive capabilities had been systematically reduced, with the EOG and RMOWU taking a lead in field operations. On a number of occasions, starting with operations in North Africa during 1942, EWE had to call on the support of Free French Sapphire teams. Even in Asia, where Axis operations were less well co-ordinated, over half of missions conducted by EWE utilised personnel from other organisations. By the end of 1943 it was apparent that EWE's role was primarily one of advising and providing passive countermeasures.

In November 1943, a report was commissioned to assess EWE's future role in occult warfare. The report was submitted in January 1944 and identified the following reasons for the challenges facing the organisation:

    a)   attrition caused by sustained operations

    b)   a recruitment crisis

    c)   tensions within the British occult community

    d)   failure to expand capabilities into fields such as psychic abilities

In November 1941, the Northern Sabbat, which had voluntarily placed itself under EWE's command, announced its independence, followed by the ICG three months later. The personnel of both had suffered significantly as a result of

Pantheon and there was significant unease at the direction then being taken by Operation Charon. While the ICG continued to co-operate with EWE, relations with the Northern Sabbat after it's withdrawal remained fractious until the end of the war. This hampered joint operations to such an extent that in September 1944, the Abwehr's *Hexenzirkel Fritz* was able to counter allied occult activities supporting Operation Market Garden. In consequence, an SS *Geisttruppen* was able to inflict losses on isolated elements of Britain's 6th Airborne, while significant disruption was caused to Allied radio networks. Only the presence of a covert RMOWU Magog detachment north of the British landing zones prevented a full-scale spirit assault.[41]

Like the Northern Sabbat and the ICG, EWE had also lost significant capabilities due to the Pantheon. Many of its seers and mystics remained unable to utilise their abilities in its aftermath, while a number remained hospitalised or seriously injured.[42] Efforts to replace these were to be hindered by recruitment to organisations such as EOG, APIB, Apollo and RMOWU. Added to this were aggressive efforts to recruit practitioners by allied occult organisations, notably DExNA, Sapphire and the AUO. The fact that both Soviet and Axis efforts to tempt personnel away from EWE enjoyed little success was scant solace. All of this was occurring at a time when unrestricted warfare and the withdrawal of many fae tribes from mortal realms were causing substantial disruption to magical energies across the globe and. Europe, however, in was particularly affected.

---

[41] Ironically this detachment included two EWE observers.

[42] The last casualty would die at a undisclosed military hospital in 1972, having remained in a coma following the operation.

The reduction of magical energy could, in part, be rectified by a greater use of psychic energies. These could be drawn on by suitable individuals with effects similar to those of magic and various schools of mysticism. The understanding of psychic energies was in its infancy and their study had been neglected by EWE. Its leadership had become complacent due to EWE's expertise in the fields of magic and mysticism. They also dramatically underestimated the disruption to magical energies that would be caused by the war. Conversely, the occult organisations of the United States, USSR and France had recognised the potential for the psychic abilities of individuals to be enhanced by technology. Such technology was frequently of extra-terrestrial or pre-human origin, but both DExNA and the CBB developed programmes intended to develop technology using existing human knowledge.

Of Britain's occult warfare organisations, only the RMOWU's 'Magog detachment' and APIB sought made significant efforts efforts to recruit personnel with significant psychic abilities. Tensions remained with APIB following EWE's actions in the aftermath of Myrddin. Furthermore APIB psychic programme utilised a number of extra-terrestrial technologies, about which EWE remained sceptical. Unlike APIB, the RMOWU's psychic Magog detachments utilised technology recovered from Atlantis, which proved more acceptable to EWE's leadership. In July 1944 EWEs R Office appointed two personnel to act as observers to Magog operations. Reports indicated the potential of psychics with technological enhancement. Particularly important were operations that took place in the Netherlands in support of Operation Market Garden. EWE's observers were embedded in a Magog team operating north of 6th Airborne's perimeter at Oosterbeek. The team was able to successfully screen itself from German sensing operations and disperse a number of *Geist* units.

Gustav Honcher of the Ahnenerbe, now promoted to general and commander of German occult operations in the Netherlands and Belgium, reported his frustrations to his superiors.

> For the first time since Normandy we have been able to gain some flexibility in occult operations. In particular we have been able to summon a number of spirits and lesser entities. These have been employed with some success against isolated enemy formations but attempts to reduce the British pocket through these means have been consistently countered.
>
> It has been impossible to launch an attack let alone concentrate spirits due to them being dissipated. It is my belief that a British coven and exorcists from the EWE organisation maybe operating within Oosterbeek and successfully screening itself from our own remote sensing. This is perplexing given the otherwise uncharacteristic inconsistency of Allied occult capability in this sector. It maybe that we are finally gaining the upper hand in the mystic field. I remain hopeful but time will tell.

Honcher had significantly overestimated the involvement of EWE in the vicinity of Oosterbeek. More astute was recognising both the poor performance of Allied occult forces (in this case due to poor co-operation) and that Allied occult capabilities were indeed starting to wane. The reality, however, was that the dominance of the Allies in occult warfare was too strong for the Germans to regain the initiative, even taking into account EWE's difficulties.

While psychic abilities offered EWE an opportunity to regain some of the capabilities that it had lost, it was clear that this was not a solution for the short term. The result was a restructure to reflect the demands placed on decreasing resources. In February 1943, C Office was merged into EACAC and its small number of flying beasts unbound. Likewise, Nedu and Styx were formerly merged into Vortigern, which also absorbed Tridamus and what remained of Cavall.

A new organisation named Obsidian was created by French, Polish and Greek occultists serving in EWE. Excalibur, theoretically consisting of non-occult capability personnel, had also been reduced by combat losses. As a result, its personnel were boosted by the temporary transfer of two RMOWU teams and an EOG unit in September 1943. The former was committed to supporting operations in North West Europe and Norway, while the latter was operated in Italy on counter lycan operations and, from October 1944, Greece. During this deployment, alongside Obsidian covens (see below), some of the earliest engagements with CBB-summoned entities would occur as part of ongoing campaigns against communist partisans. In January 1945, the RMOWU teams were reassigned from EWE's command for operations in the Baltic. The EOG unit remained under EWE command until the end of the war. Deployed to Southern China in April 1945 it played a crucial role in hunting down the dragons intended to be awoken as part of Japan's Operation Furaribi.

To further enhance its forces, EWE initiated a programme intended to utilise army and navy commandos who would be mind-wiped after operations. Despite the objections of AREBAC this was nonetheless implemented from January 1944. EWE was also known to have covertly terminated a number of army personnel who had co-operated with Excalibur on particularly sensitive operations. The director of R- Office, Algernon Wynn, authorised these operations and noted in a report to EWE's leadership

What is the loss of a few dozen soldiers in a war? The padres [AREBAC] won't know if it was Nazis bullets or British ones in the skulls. Much better than risking a memory returning, for both them and operational security. We have made too many offerings to devils these past years for any of us to become fastidious over such things.

Occult operations were underpinned by a fear of hysteria, panic and the persecution of practitioners if activities became known to the general public. Thus the eradication of risks to 'operational security' remained a concern to both sides during and after the war.

The termination of untrained personnel who witnessed occult operations became more common as Allied forces advanced rapidly through France in the summer of 1944. On August 18, one of the largest events of this kind took place northeast of Nimes. A joint Obsidian-Excalibur unit was attempting to disrupt an Ahnenerbe ceremony to contact

Baphomet. This was taking place within a subterranean temple complex when a firefight erupted at the temple entrance. During this time, a SAS unit returning from an unrelated mission intervened, having identified the defenders as SS due to their uniforms and presuming the attackers to be from a British or partisan unit. By the time the defenders at the entrance had been overwhelmed, the coven within the temple had managed to summon a servitor of Baphomet. The creature promptly slew two of the SAS and severely injured an Obsidian seer before it was dismissed. The remaining six SAS personnel were terminated as a precaution.[43]

The declining military position of Germany enabled Excalibur to conduct operations aimed at retrieving artefacts. The purpose was to increase British capabilities (particularly those of EWE), prevent their use by German resistance groups and ensure that they were not acquired by the United States, France, the Soviets or even fae or extra-terrestrial forces. There was also an increasing suspicion that potentially hostile extra-terrestrials would also seek to acquire them. R Office had responsibility for co-ordinating the retrieval of artefacts, which from November 1944 was given the codename Operation Malice. Prior to this, retrieval operations had been ad hoc and conducted as required. From the winter of 1944, a list of fifty artefacts considered to be 'of high priority and special significance' was created for Excalibur's attention.

---

[43] An undisclosed number of British bombers are also believed to have fallen to C-Flight Mosquitos following encounters with flying weres and alien craft.

A small number of the artefacts targeted by Malice had been misidentified as archaeological anomalies or curiosities. Frequently held in museums or the private collections of Nazis officials, they were lightly guarded, if at all and easily retrieved by Excalibur teams. Amongst the most significant of these artefacts was a navigation system from a Vimana flying craft in March 1945, known as the *'Steiner Discs'*.

The discs had been recovered from a temple complex in the Indian region of Rajputana by a team of US archaeologists in 1919. Mistakenly identified as carvings of a creation story, they were sold to a Nazis official in 1934, who gifted them to another party member in 1940. R Office had become interested in the artefact when, in 1936, they acquired sketches made by an artist who had travelled with the US archaeological team. EWE commissioned its own expedition to the temple complex in 1941 and concluded that the artefact had not only been misidentified but likely represented an unusually intact system from the craft. By this time, EWE had no way of identifying the whereabouts of the artefact. In 1944 it had been theorised that the artefact may have been activated by the Ahnenerbe to serve as a guidance system aboard the V-1 flying bomb, although the inaccuracy of the weapon soon disproved this.

It is likely that the artefact would have remained hidden had it not been for a brief study commenced by the SS Black Sun organisation. This had commenced in late May 1944, following a chance visit by SS Major Gustav Steiner to the owner's house during a Nazis Party function. Steiner had recognised the nature of the artefact but could not complete his investigation due to being deployed to Normandy two weeks later in response to the Allied invasion. The major was part of an SS coven captured south of Bayeux by an EOG team and his papers passed to EWE who were able to determine the location of the artefact. It was thus one of the first objects added to the Malice list.

In February 1945, the artefact was recovered from the residence of a former Nazis Dienstleiter (service leader) east of Dortmund. The operation encountered no opposition as the official and his family had fled but was nonetheless considered a significant success. This was due to the rarity of the object (the most complete example of its kind recovered until 1985) and the fact that a French Sapphire team arrived two days later in search of it.[44]

The majority of activities conducted under Operation Malice were not as bloodless. Many of the artefacts identified were held in guarded facilities by German occult organisations. These were almost invariably located with mountain ranges or heavily forested areas, as far as possible from major settlements. Locations not only provided better security but also access to stronger magical energies associated with nature. Mystics, creatures, spirits and entities of various types were also used to provide protection for these facilities. The result was that Excalibur was compelled to call on similar support. In consequence, the most intense occult battles were to occur in the wilds of Germany during 1945. Germany's occult units emerged victorious in many of these engagements despite a rapidly deteriorating military situation. The resilience of Germany's occult forces had taken those of the West by surprise. This surprise had rapidly turned to frustration. On March 29, the director of R Office,

---

[44] The artefact was finally reactivated in 1997 and remains in a secure NATO facility beneath Greenland.

Algernon Wynn, wrote to EWE's leadership criticising what he perceived to be the failings Excalibur:

> The enemy are in full flight in some sectors, with fronts collapsing. Allied armies are across the Rhine. Our air forces control the skies. Yet we remain unable to raid museums.

Wynn was over-optimistic in his appraisal of the strategic situation. Operation Plunder, the crossing of the Rhine, had only happened six days before. Wynn was rebuked by EWE's leadership, who by now fully appreciated the crisis facing them.

It had been anticipated that a deteriorating conventional military situation would be reflected in Germany's occult forces. The capabilities of these forces had been diminished but they had not collapsed. This was because, like many occult organisations, those of Nazis Germany had operated at the fringes of the state and society. This made them less vulnerable to declining national fortunes, circumstances recognised by Allied occultists as it was the basis of their own existence. The failure was to recognise the benefits to German occult forces of closer ties to their military.

German occult forces were only integrated with the conventional military to a very limited degree but this was anathema to occultists in Western Europe and North America. Such a situation was perceived as being detrimental to effective occult warfare. It was perceived as increasing the risk of revealing the existence of the occult to the general populace, while it was feared co-operation with conventional military forces would impact flexibility. The

Ahnenerbe, Black Sun and others succeeded in maintaining full independence while benefitting from military resources. Thus, the Todt Labor Organisation unknowingly constructed bunker complexes that would be used to house these organisations. Added to this was a significant supply of military equipment, such as small arms and heavier weapons, available to the occult forces of Nazis Germany. Notably, Black Sun maintained a force of light armoured vehicles that were used in all theatres to support covens operating near the frontlines.

The only occult organisation of the Allies that came near to the capability of Black Sun was APIB's C Flight. Even the relatively well-resourced organisations of the United States had little intrinsic military capability. In such cases, conventional military hardware or resources had to be commandeered on an ad hoc basis. It was a shortcoming that was not apparent until the final months of the war, when engagements become more common and involved units of up to platoon strength. The result was that Excalibur and similar organisations were outgunned in conventional military terms and deficient in occult capability. The specialist training of the Excalibur teams could never replace the capabilities of mystically trained occult warfare units. With British occult resources over extended it was now that EWE needed the support of its foreign allies. Unfortunately, this occurred at a time of increasing rivalry that lead to a decline in co-operation. Increasing both US and French occult forces sought to retrieve artefacts held by the Germans. There was also evidence of growing frustration with British occult warfare activities in general. The head of the AUO's Baltic operations section wrote to his Sapphire counterpart in February 1945 that:

> The British need to recognise that the old ways have been swept away. The age of the warlock is over. The path to mastery is not the traditional mystic route but an amalgam of old and new. Recklessness has exposed us to many new threats and now is the time for unity within occult circles and not a hording of knowledge.

This was a situation of EWE's own making. Through its growing influence it had began to symbolise Britain's occult warfare. Its unwillingness to accept new ideas made it appear outdated, while the likes of operations Charon and Pantheon had gained it a reputation of irresponsibility.

Of the 36 operations launched as part of Malice between January and May 1945, only 21 achieved their objectives. EWE's remaining occult forces were also significantly eroded. By April 1945 Vortigern contained only 15 creatures, a combination of Barghests and lycans. A report by EWE's strategic planning committee report concluded on April 15 that:

> We must contend with the fact that those entities, and indeed creatures, that are more easily bound have been so, and thus likely exterminated or released from further services by pacts. It is no longer possible to effectively bind or summon new entities due to continued loses and the diversion of resources to support the marine leviathan campaign. Further

to this the remaining pool of viable creatures and entities is rapidly diminishing due to wartime activities by the enemy and our allies. It is likely that our occult forces will experience a complete collapse by September given the current tempo of operations. It is strongly recommended that Malice be curtailed.

A consequence of the report was the creation of contingencies to be implemented if EWE was unable to continue to bind its existing commanded entities. These contingencies were combined findings from Operations Trebuchet and Portcullis. Codenamed Lethe, the resulting protocols remain highly classified and form the basis of certain NATO and British occult contingency plans.

On May 5 1945, the penultimate day of the war in Europe, Operation Medusa was launched. It was the largest operation undertaken as part of Malice and proved to be EWEs final operation in the European theatre. The size of Medusa was due to it using forces drawn from Excalibur and a supporting SAS unit (which was subsequently terminated). This was necessitated by occult forces being unavailable due to operational requirements. Principally, these requirements included activities by Vortigern against German forces in Scandinavia and Bavaria, whilst assets were also deployed against Soviet CBB units in the Balkans and Middle East. Medusa's target was a collection of biological samples extracted from the remains of large humanoids located by Black Sun operatives. The samples were a late addition to the Malice target list, EWE's interest having been piqued by CBB activities to acquire them in February 1945. The remains were known to have been located by a joint Ahnenerbe-Black Sun team in a pyramid buried beneath Western Bulgaria in 1944. There was some disagreement in Allied occult circles over the precise nature of the remains. DExNA favoured an extra-terrestrial link, while both EWE and France's Sapphire proposed they were likely the result of Nephilim settlement in pre-human Europe.

As in the case of the *Steiner Discs* that May, there was a clear desire to deprive both the Nazis and other Allied powers of the target artefacts. The commander of the Excalibur team was instructed:

> Destruction is required in case acquisition by enemy or other parties is threatened. Retrieval is to be considered only a concomitant advantage of this operations. Authorisation is given for proactive action against enemy and other parties to prevent acquisition of artefacts.

'Other parties' was a term referring to either Soviet or French occult teams operating in Germany with the intention of retrieving artefacts. A number of engagements were reported between EWE teams and CBB groups. While more capable than their Soviet counterparts, it was frequently the case that the EWE teams withdrew due to the risk of casualties. In consequence, an undisclosed number of artefacts were destroyed to prevent their capture by the CBB in the closing weeks of the war. Less common were engagements between British and French occult units, but a handful of incidents were reported to have occurred in Indo-China, central Africa and southern Germany during 1945.

Invariably units withdrew before serious fighting but a number of French lycans and EWE mystics were killed in an engagement at a temple on the Thai border in June 1945.

Ultimately, Medusa proved to be only a partial success. The samples were destroyed by the team on route to their link-up with British forces. A report on the operation concluded:

> Enemy defenses were in disarray and the defending were-detachment easily overcame. The as yet unidentified entity at the site was contained... Red ambush east of rendezvous was repulsed but the containers were destroyed to prevent loss. Red forces then retired. SAS unit was exterminated in contact with enemy lycans. Enemy occult strength now at low ebb and showing signs of collapse with magic streams seemingly untapped even in close vicinity of target complex. Increasing activity by Soviet occult units, notably CBB, now poses a greater risk to further Malice operations. It is recommended that if contact with Soviet forces is anticipated, as it is likely to be the case in future operations in this region, Vortigern detachments are assigned. Co-operation with, and subsequent termination of, conventional military units remains viable with sufficient support, providing their loses can be sustained. There is little evidence of significant mystic or psychic capability being employed effectively by CBB operatives in the field but they demonstrate a growing capacity to do so.

It was an inglorious end to EWE operations in Europe but one that foreshadowed conflicts with Soviet occult forces in the years that followed.

197

Chapter 10

The Occult War: Secrecy, Countermeasure and Offence

In September, Britain's occult warfare strategy had three key objectives:

1. countering enemy occult operations
2. enhancing the capabilities of British and Allied conventional forces
3. ensuring occult warfare activities did not become common knowledge

In broad terms, these were goals shared with the occult warfare organisations of Allied and enemy nations.

Effective countermeasures against enemy occult operations were a prerequisite if British occult forces were to effectively support their conventional counterparts. That this was achieved is evident by the fact that the Axis powers were never able to fully exploit the potential of their own occult capabilities. Initiatives to utilise spirits, lycans and marine leviathans to significantly influence combat were consistently thwarted. Localised successes were achieved, but these were largely contained by British and Allied occult units. The result was that the deployment of both British and Axis occult warfare units nullified opposing capabilities. This prevented British occult units from participating directly in combat operations, but this was never the intended outcome. An example were the operations by British marine Leviathans. These efficiently countered Axis ambitions in that field while never employed in significant strength against conventional enemy naval vessels. Operation Tridamus was a notable exception in British occult warfare, as it was policy to utilise units such as Excalibur, EOG, RMOWU and APIB's C Flight for combat roles.

The keystone of British occult warfare was not battlefield capability but mystics, seers and other users of magical energy. The only notable deficiency was in psychic capabilities. Only the RMOWU and APIB possessed significant capabilities in this field. These capabilities, however, compared unfavourably to those of US, French and Soviet occult organisations. British occult forces, and EWE in particular, had at their disposal a vast pool of mystic and esoteric resources. This included artefacts such as Mjolnir and the Kaladanda that were acquired during the war. Due to the need to analyse and activate such artefacts, they had little short term impact. Nevertheless, possessing artefacts prevented their use by the enemy and offered the potential to enhance occult warfare operations. Through pooling resources for projects such as Operations Monolith and Trebuchet British capabilities were further enhanced.

Despite resource sharing, as resources became depleted or overstretched by operational demands, deficiencies began to become significant. Operations Portcullis and Drawbridge began as British operations but relied on US, Dutch and French support. It was fortunate for the British occult war effort that by this time, the capabilities of APIB, ICG and EOG had expanded sufficiently to sustain operations. Even if EWE had been attrited to the point of collapsed in 1945, it is likely Britain's occult war effort would have continued, albeit less effectively.

The great strength of Britain's occult warfare, and indeed that of other Allied nations, lay in the depth of mystical resources that could be called upon. Through their empires, the British, Dutch and French could call upon practitioners from a diverse array of traditions. This included Celtic, South Pacific, North American, African and South Asian disciplines. Whilst any individual could become a skilled practitioner in such arts, those from the cultures from which these traditions originated were considered to be most effective.

It was not uncommon for Allied mystical activities to be supported by mystics drawn from two, three or even more disciplines. This allowed allied offensive and defensive mystical activities to use subtle, overlapping wards and enchantments. The occult war was not a one-sided conflict and the Germans were able to achieve success. The more limited range of resources available dictated a less subtle application of rites and enchantments that relied on their sheer power. These could, however, be exhausted by the Allies responding rapidly to change the wards that they used. Nazis racial policies in Eastern Europe exacerbated the Allied advantage. Hundreds of potential mystics were incarcerated, murdered or turned against the occupiers. This included Roma practitioners, whose control of hexes could have proved crucial.

Allied mystical capabilities ensured enemy occult operations could be disrupted. This could include limiting remote sensing such as scrying or, conversely, facilitating more effective remote sensing activities against the Axis. Allied mystics also had at their disposal greater options for using wards, sigils and other means to disrupt entities and spirits. These capabilities were also used to expedite Operation Charon. Another significant advantage enjoyed by British occult organisations over those of the Axis was inter Allied co-operation. This never reached the levels of that between the conventional military forces of the Allied powers. Within Allied occult circles, the British, with the exception of the RMOWU and later APIB, had a reputation for embracing traditional ideas while disregarding new understanding. They were perceived as recklessly applying this through high-risk projects such as Operations Cavall, Trebuchet and Pantheon. The result was suspicion and mistrust of British motivations.

The period of January to September 1945 saw intense competition for control of the occult artefacts and knowledge held by the Axis. Nonetheless, despite occasional clashes between occult forces, co-operation between the occult groups of the Allied nations was significantly more than that which existed within the Axis. France had jealously guarded the discoveries it made in Atlantis, but by 1940, co-operation had increased to a significant degree. The relationship remained tense, hostile at times, but the sharing of personnel and knowledge continued throughout the war. Co-operation with DExNA and other US agencies was more effective and resulted in joint research activities within US borders, including Prairie Monarch.

Conversely the German occult war effort was hampered by continual inter-service rivalries. The Ahnenerbe in particular refused to share tomes that would have enhanced the capabilities of O.Abt.K, Walküre and Black Sun in particular. Nazis occult operations were further hampered by political interference by the influential Thule Society. Italian activities were better co-ordinated and more focused but there was little co-ordination with German activities.

Occult diplomacy was to have been a key element of Britain's occult strategy. Operation Tidal Wave commenced pre-war and was the most effective diplomatic initiative of its kind, the protocols of which remain active. Despite this, success was inconsistent and this was to have far-reaching implications. The attempt to obtain the co-operation of vampires through Taurus ultimately failed through poor intelligence. Heavy-handed initial efforts served to alienate many fae and mer lords. French actions against the faes of Brittany in 1940, and failed Axis diplomacy, ensured the fae in general sought to avoid overt involvement in what they perceived as a conflict between humans. Consequentially many tribes and kingdoms opted for friendly neutrality, with a handful actively participating or supplying mercenaries, sometimes to both sides. Fae willingness to support Operation Portcullis was an example of how diplomatic success could be achieved within limited objectives.

Britain had few diplomatic missions assigned to extra-terrestrials. This persisted until APIB took the lead role in this. German efforts in this field would have been significant had it not been for the intransigence of many extra-terrestrial races. Many such races viewed earth as a backwater that could be used as a pawn in their own conflicts. When the potential rewards of extra-terrestrial co-operation became more attainable Britain was fortunate to be able to co-operate with DExNA.

In regard to maintaining the secrecy of its occult operations Britain employed many of the means utilised by the Axis. There remains no official recognition as witnesses were exterminated, cover-ups made, mind wiped or individuals ridiculed. Greater understanding of psychology enabled sightings of creatures and other phenomena to be dismissed as stress of mass hallucination. Improvements in technology also enabled individual happenings that would have been previously been attributed to witchcraft or similar to be explained through science. Post war, a number of successful programmes have enabled the truth to be discredited as conspiracy theories, pseudoscience or other ideologies. This maintenance of secrecy was the greatest achievement of Britain's occult war. World War II has passed into history as a war won by sacrifice and heroism. This enabled organisations such as EWE and APIB to continue to operate in secrecy as the world transitioned from a World War to a Cold War.

APPENDIX 1

British occult organisations
Italics denotes historical organisation

Exotic Warfare Executive	
Section	**Role**
Central Committee	Directing Operations
M Office	Maritime Operations
G Office	Psychic infiltration
C Office (later EACAC)	Aerial warfare
R Office	Artefacts
H office	Internal security
E Office.	Mystic and extra-terrestrial diplomatic relations
Excalibur	Field Operations
General Defence Group	Co-ordination of occult defence activity
Nedu group	Counter spirit operations, mystic counter measures
Styx group	Counter spirit operations, mystic counter measures

Other British Occult Organisations	
Organisation	**Affiliation**
APIB	*RAF*
Apollo/OOE/SOEAS	*SOE*
AREBaC	*Anglican Church*
EOG	*British Army*
Guinevere	*MI5*
ICG	Independent
Magog	RMOWU
Northern Sabbat	Independent
RMOWU	*Royal Navy/Marines*
Vortigern	Independent

APPENDIX 2

Allied occult organisations
Italics denotes historical organisation

French Gemstone Departments		
Section	**Affiliation**	**Role**
Ruby	*Navy*	Maritime operations, security of Atlantis
Emerald	*Army-Navy*	Mystical intelligence gathering.
Sapphire	*Army*	Mystic warfare
Jade	*Navy/Air Force*	Study of Extra-terrestrials
Onyx	*Navy*	Diplomatic relations with the fae and contacts with entities

Other Allied Occult Organisations		
Organisation	**Affiliation**	**Role**
AUO	*Dutch Navy*	Occult warfare
CBB	Independent	Occult warfare
Ocean Monarch	*US Navy*	Marine leviathans
Prairie Wendigo	*US Army*	Occult warfare
Prairie Emperor	*US Army*	Summoning and binding
Sovereign	US Navy	Occult warfare
Thunder Eagle	*USAAF*	Occult warfare
UAMS	Sapphire	Lycan warfare
Vyriy	*Soviet Navy*	Occult warfare

APPENDIX 3

Axis occult organisations
Italics denotes historical organisation

German Organisations		
Section	Affiliation	Role
Ahnenerbe	*SS*	Occult intelligence and research
Black Sun	*SS*	Occult research, extra-terrestrial operations
Btl.SJ	*Wehrmacht*	Occult creatures
Gebirgswächter	*SS*	Mountain warfare and counter insurgency
Gruppe Heimdall	*SS*	Far East operations
SS.BdN	*SS*	Occult creatures
SS.Kp.K	*SS*	Lycan and were warfare
NZL	*Luftwaffe*	Occult creatures
Lurwitz	*SS*	Occult diplomacy
O.Abt.K	*Kriegsmarine*	Occult maritime operations
Thule Society	Independent	Occult operations
Wotan	*SS*	Spirit warfare
Walküre	*Luftwaffe*	Occult operations

Other Axis Occult Organisations		
Organisation	Affiliation	Role
Caelus	Independent	Extra-terrestrial diplomacy
Fūten	IJA	Occult warfare
Trident	Italian Navy	Maritime warfare
Yōkai	IJN	Occult warfare

APPENDIX 4

Occult operation, project and programme codenames referred to in A Hidden War

Codename	Nation	Years	Purpose
Arctic Panther	SOVIET UNION	1945-9	Covens at sea
Artemis	Britain	1925-39	Deployment of Barghests
Boatman	Britain	1944-5	Contingency for collapse of occult forces
Blood Raven	France	1940-5	Relocation of French resources
Bronzepfeil	Germany	1940-4	Bombing enhancement
Castiel	Britain	1926-31	Counter entity tactics
Cavall	Britain	1938-43	Barghest operations
Charon	Britain	1940-7	Contacts with entities
Deflector	USA	1943-7	Screening trials
Drawbridge	Britain	1944-6	Counter Die Glocke
Furaribi	Japan	1944-5	Dragon operations
Ice Bolt	Soviet	1941-3	Weather manipulation
Kinati	USA	1943-5	Bombing enhancement
Lilith	Italy	1928-43	Occult creatures
Linesman	Britain	1943	Acquisition od artefacts
Luison	Britain	1934-9	Barghests and Holy sites
Malice	Britain	1944-6	Artefact recovery
Medusa	Britain	1945	Artefact recovery
Myrrdin	Britain	1935-9	Dragon operations
Noden	Germany	1942-5	Advanced U-boats
Ossaert	Netherlands	1940	Evacuation of resources
Pantheon	Britain	1940	Defence of Dunkirk
Portcullis	Britain	1944-5	Counter Die Glocke
Red-Bat	Anglo-US	1943-4	Binding the Thunderbird
Shetland	Britain	1940	Binding a seedrache

Silver Shard	Germany	1939–45	Counter lycan contingency
Sky Cage	Britain	1944–	Counter extra-terrestrial operations
Southern Storm	Britain	1940–5	Elemental warfare
Sturmschild	Germany	1940	Acquisition of Mjolnir
Talos	Britain	1941	Counter flying beasts and later extra-terrestrials
Trebuchet	Britain	1940–	Counter entity tactics
Tidal Wave	Britain	1936–45	Diplomatic mission to the Mers
Tridamus	Britain	1938–43	Spirit and entity warfare
Vel	Germany	1941–5	Bombing enhancement
Winchester	USA	1918–?	Counter entity and creature tactics
Wotan	Germany	1938	Valkyrie research

Index

B

C

F

O

P

T

U